# THE QUEST FOR A TREASURE MAP

*By Debbra M. Long*

Order this book online at www.trafford.com
or email orders@trafford.com

Most Trafford titles are also available at major online book retailers.



Printed in Victoria, BC, Canada.

ISBN: 978-1-4251-8802-3

*Our mission is to efficiently provide the world's finest, most comprehensive book publishing service, enabling every author to experience success. To find out how to publish your book, your way, and have it available worldwide, visit us online at www.trafford.com/10510*

*Trafford rev. 11/11/2009*

www.trafford.com

**North America & international**
toll-free: 1 888 232 4444 (USA & Canada)
phone: 250 383 6864 • fax: 812 355 4082

*To My dad*
*Charles F. Obert*
*A man who loved adventure*

## CHAPTER 1

*Debbie smiled* as she left the house and headed off to work, she owns the local Library. As she approached the steps to the Library driving up in their motor home and honking, Al and Karen stopped and opened the door. "Hi!" Debbie waved, as she walked over to the motor home. "Heading out for a camping trip?" She giggled.

Al and Karen laughed, "No" Al exclaimed, "We are going to see my mother, she wants help with her spring cleaning."

Karen chimed in, "We were hoping to catch you before you got to work this morning. I told Al we should let you know where we were going."

Debbie smiled, "I'm glad you did, I would have worried if I hadn't heard from you. Have a safe trip and we'll see you when you return. When are you coming back?" Debbie questioned.

Al and Karen looked at each other and shrugged their shoulders. Al thought for a moment and then added, "Maybe in four days, I can't stay away very long. I have to much work to do."

Debbie laughed, "Okay, Al, you two have fun, even if it is cleaning for your mom. See you later." Debbie waved good-bye as they shut the door of the motor home and took off. She watched as they disappeared down the street and out of town.

When Al and Karen arrived at his mother's place, she was excited to see them, and of course, put Al right to work. She had many jobs for Al and Karen, but the most important to her was cleaning the fruit cellar. Mabel, Al's mom, had wanted to clear out the fruit cellar for months and was anxious to get started. The fruit cellar hadn't been totally cleaned out for years. Al got right to work on the cellar, and was making great progress. He found his mother had done some strange things like wrapping all her canned goods in old newspaper and whatever else she could find to use. "Mom!" Al called up from the cellar, "Why did you wrap all your canned jars in paper ... and stuff?" he asked in frustration.

She replied, "I wanted to protect them that's why! Go ahead and take all the paper off and throw it away."

"You mean you don't want to protect them anymore?" Al just shook his head and proceeded to take all the paper off and throw it away. He soon realized many of the jars were dated as far back as 1890. He hollered up the stairs again. "Are all these jars yours mom?"

Mabel and Karen came down the stairs to the cellar. "No!" Mabel snatched a jar from Al's hand. "Some were my mothers and I just kept them. Don't ask me why. Just throw them away and the cellar will be done faster." Mabel patted her son on the shoulder and headed up the steep stairs. As she made her way up the narrow stairs she grumbled, "At my age why would I care about this stuff."

After a couple hours Al was almost done when he came across a jar wrapped in a thin skin. He took it upstairs to show his mom and get a better look at it. To Al's surprise, the material was a piece of thin leather with some strange markings on it. Al asked his mother about it and she said it was nothing, she had found it when they dug out the earth to make the fruit cellar shortly after they had moved into the house. Mabel said she wrapped the jar with it cause she had run out of paper. Al asked if he could have it. His mom scowled at him, "What do you want with a piece of dirty old garbage? I am trying to throw all that garbage away and you want to keep it. When you get to be my age, you'll wonder why you saved half the junk you saved. If you think you have to have it, go ahead, but I tell you its garbage!" She scowled at him, and then hugged him. "Thank you for helping your old mom."

Al thanked his mother for the piece of leather and finished the jobs she had for him to do. That night he showed the piece of leather to Karen.

They were both fascinated by the markings, and then Karen noted it to be a map. "Al, I think this is a map! Not like a map with mountains and roads but a map using symbols only." (Women notice these things.)

Al examined the leather with its strange markings. "You could be right, Karen." Al studied the markings on the map. " Karen, these markings could very well be of Native American origin."

Karen suggested they call Dave & Debbie to see what they had to say about it. "Dave & Debbie are Native American, so maybe they would know something about the markings on the map." Al got his cell phone and started to make the call when Karen yelled, "Stop! Use the landline. Someone could listen in on your conversation." Al agreed and used the landline.

Al called Dave, but there was no answer. "What do we do now Karen?"

Karen thought for a moment, "Lets go to Canyon Lake Lodge and keep trying to call them. It's a good place to meet without being disturbed. We'll stay one night in the Lodge and use a landline to call them. What do you think?"

Al scratched his head in thought, "We could just use a pay phone."

Karen got up and started packing to leave. "Al, the pay phone is to public for the call you need to make. We need to stay one night for a private phone call. Maybe not even a night, just check into a room, make a call and go stay in our motor home after that."

Al looked at Karen as she packed and talked. "Are you nuts! Do you realize what we would be paying for that room? We don't need to make that expensive a call!" Al started gathering his things. He looked up at Karen in frustration. "I'll use the pay phone in the lodge and you can keep people away. It'll be private enough, maybe. Al shook his head, "Okay, I'm feeling some concern about this map. What if it's nothing or what if it is something big? Do you suppose someone alive knows of its existence?"

"No. Your mom dug it up when she dug out her fruit cellar. No one knows of its existence. If by chance someone did know of this piece of leather, and by chance it is a map, then they would have been looking for it all these years. Then we wouldn't have the map someone else would." Karen replied. "Are we going to Canyon Lake Lodge or not?"

"Yes, lets go now. Mom thinks we are leaving now so we shouldn't disappoint her." Al packed up his things and started for their motor home, with Karen close behind. They said good-bye to Al's mom and off they went.

# CHAPTER 2

*It took* all night to get to Canyon Park. Upon entering the Park, Al and Karen were so tired they decided to pull over somewhere and take a nap.

When they woke up it was two o'clock in the afternoon. Al was amazed they had slept so long. Arriving at Canyon Lake Lodge, Al had a change of mind, "I think we should check into a room even if it is just to make a call."

Karen smiled but said nothing. They checked in promptly and hurried up to their room.

Al used the telephone in the room to call Dave. "Hello, Dave I have been trying to get a hold of you since yesterday." Al paused, giving Karen a strange look.

Karen looked puzzled at Al, "What is it?" she whispered.

Al held up his index finger and whispered, "just a minute." Then he proceeded to tell Dave about finding the old piece of leather. He was pausing quite often, then reluctantly told Dave he thought it might be an old map. Karen decided something was wrong, but listened to Al explain the map to Dave. Then Al quit talking and just listened, Dave told Al not to say anything else until he got back home to Mobil Park City.

"I think someone is listening in on this conversation, Dave." Al was becoming anxious, "I feel uneasy about coming home right now, I would like it better if you and Debbie came to meet us."

Al insisted on Dave coming to Canyon Lake Lodge, so he agreed to come. "Don't worry Al, I'll meet you at Canyon Lake Lodge. Debbie and I will be there in about an hour and a half. Be careful, Al. We'll hurry." Dave reassured him. Al was glad Dave was coming and hung up the phone.

Karen looked concerned, "Who was listening, Al?"

"I don't know." Al replied pacing the floor. "We need to put all our things in the motor home and be prepared to leave quickly. Uh…the map, we need to put it in a safe place, but where?" Al was anxious for Dave to arrive. "It should only take Dave and Debbie an hour and a half to get here. If we can hold out that long we'll be okay." Al reassured Karen as well as himself.

"Al, what do we do with the map while we are waiting?" Karen urged.

Al stared long and hard at Karen, "I don't know…. I don't know!" Al turned and walked to the door, then stopped. Suddenly he wheeled around, "I have it!"

Karen looked startled, "You have what?" This was frustrating Karen, and she was concerned about someone listening in on the conversation. Especially when she suggested he use a landline to avoid just that… someone listening in on the conversation. Soon Karen was pacing the floor with Al. "How would anyone know to listen in on your conversation? We are ordinary people. No one special, and no one knows, or did know, we found this strange map. So why?" She looked inquisitively at Al for an answer. Al was deep in thought and barely heard what she said. "Al! What do you think?"

"What! Think about what?" Al was agitated and still trying to think of what to do to protect the map.

"Never mind." Karen said in frustration. She knew she had to help Al find a resolution for the map and soon. "I know, hide it in your shoe or sock."

Al scowled at Karen. "What if they make me take my shoes and socks off?" Shaking his head he continued pacing.

"Oh, I didn't think about them stripping us." Karen looked scared and even more concerned. "I hope Dave and Debbie hurry. Should we seek out a crowd and mingle? Maybe no one will bother us if we are among other people." Karen encouraged.

Al shook his head, "No, not until I figure out what to do about the map. I think we are safer here in the room. Also Dave knows where we are."

Karen scowled, "So does whoever it was that was listening to us... Duh! What if they decide to come up here and get the map from us?"

"They won't! Not unless they are Native American or know someone who is." Al was suddenly confident. "We'll just sit tight until help arrives."

After about an hour, Al decided they needed to go down to the lobby and get something to eat, again the dilemma of the map. Al wasn't sure what to do with it. After studying the room for the past hour he discovered a place he could stash the map and it would be virtually undetected.

Karen studied the situation, "What if they find it Al?"

"It took me an hour to discover the place and I don't think we will give anyone longer than that to study the situation. Besides there's a good chance that if anyone wanted the map they would think we had it on our person not stashed in this room somewhere." Al opened the door. "Let's go eat."

Karen got her purse and marched out the door with Al close behind. Once down in the lobby, they stopped and observed everyone in sight. "Does anyone look like they know who we are?" Al whispered to Karen.

Karen glanced around, "No, actually it doesn't seem threatening at all."

Al walked over to the window, "I'm going to call Dave and see where he is." Karen walked toward the gift shop and looked around observing people. By the door she stopped and looked out toward the lobby. Karen watched Al over by the window and glancing around she noticed the clerk watching Al. Maybe it was a coincidence, then the clerk looked at her. When Karen looked right at the clerk, the clerk acted suspicious and disappeared into the office. Karen's heart quickened and she rushed over to Al who had just hung up the phone after talking to Dave.

"Al, I think I know who was listening in on your conversation." Karen whispered. "Did you get a hold of Dave?"

"Yes, I talked to Dave. They will be here in about fifteen minutes and we'll meet them in the restaurant." Al said quietly. "Who do you think was listening?"

Karen and Al walked over to the restaurant. "I think it was the clerk that checked us in earlier. She was watching you pretty close when you walked over to the window to call Dave, and she acted suspicious when she saw me watching her." Karen thought for a moment, "I wonder what made her decide to listen in on your conversation?"

Al looked across the lobby toward the front desk and observed the clerk watching them again. "I don't know but she is watching us again so you may be right about her. I'll feel better when Dave joins us and we get out of here." Karen and Al were seated, and waited for Dave and Debbie to arrive.

Karen sat nervously twitching her fingers and watching the people around the room. Al slowly took Karen's hand in his and quietly said, "Don't look now but I could swear that someone from Mobil Park City is in this room right now." Al smiled at Karen, "act natural and smile back at me like we are having a normal conversation." Karen smiled and leaned toward Al.

"Who is it you think you see, Al." Karen whispered.

Al glanced past Karen and said, "I'm not sure but maybe it's Gene. He's wearing a weird wig and mustache, glasses and a hat." Al looked back at Karen, "Why would Gene be here wearing a disguise?"

The waiter came to the table to take their order and Karen turned to talk to the waiter. This gave her an opportunity to look toward the guy Al had recognized. Karen turned quickly back to Al. Al told the waiter they were waiting for someone to join them and so they would wait to order, the waiter left. "Al, it does look like Gene in a disguise! What do you think?" Karen was getting pretty shook by now.

Al smiled, "Don't worry anymore, Dave and Debbie are here." Karen turned and saw them walking to the table. What a relief, Karen was so happy to see them, Al too.

Dave and Debbie sat down and quickly noticed the stress that Karen and Al were under. Dave shook Al's hand "Don't worry anymore we're here."

Al told Dave about the clerk watching them and Gene in a disguise across the room. Dave carefully scanned the room. "It does look like Gene!" Dave observed. "I don't think his presence is a coincidence, and the disguise is definitely strange. Has he talked to anyone you know of?" Al told Dave he hadn't seen him talk to anyone except the waiter. Dave instructed Karen to watch Gene while Al and him looked at the map.

"The map isn't with us, Dave." Al stated.

Dave took a pen out of his pocket and scribbled something on a napkin. "Just pretend to show me and let's see who we have watching us." Dave smiled at Al.

Al agreed and pulled a brown paper out of his pocket and placed it on the table. Dave pulled it close but didn't lift it up. Karen got excited, " Oh, I think Gene is interested in our activity!"

"Don't worry" Dave encouraged. "Let's have something to eat and then we will go get the map." They ordered and had a nice visit in spite of the underlying circumstances surrounding them.

After dinner, Al and Karen took Dave and Debbie up to their room to get the map. Upon entering their room they discovered there had been a visitor while they were out. The room had been turned upside down. It was quite apparent that someone was looking for the map. The question was who and how did they know about it in the first place. Al closed the door; "what if this place is bugged?" questioned Karen.

"It's not likely the room is bugged but just in case be quiet." Dave said carefully. Al retrieved the map from its hiding place. Dave held his finger up to his mouth to quiet everyone from saying anything. Al carefully opened the door after collecting all their belongings that had been left in the room. Dave checked the hallway to see if it was clear and they vacated quickly.

Once outside by the motor home, they gasped for air. "Dave don't panic, but I think I saw two more residence from Mobil Park City standing on the stairwell when we ran out the door." Debbie noted.

"Yes, I saw them. It was kind of sketchy but they looked like a disguised Marlene and Norma." Dave unlocked the motor home and they all went in. "Let's have a look at the map, Al." Al pulled the leather out of his pocket and laid it on the table. Debbie pulled all the curtains and Karen locked the door. Then they all examined the mysterious piece of old leather.

"This is definitely a map, however it is only half of a map." Dave proclaimed.

Karen anxiously pointed out that the map wasn't like a map at all. "It looks more like instructions." Karen said anxiously.

Dave shook his head, "No, it's designed to fool most people. The markings are definitely of Native American origin. What tribe, I'm not sure of yet but the pictures are hieroglyphics from the seventeen, eighteen hundreds. It looks like the map was split intentionally. Probably to insure the safety of the treasure." Dave carefully pointed out the ragged edge of the thin leather. "I can't be sure, but it looks like a piece was torn off here."

Al scratched his head, "Where do you think the other half is?"

"I don't know, are you sure there wasn't another piece in the cellar at your mom's house?" Dave asked as he studied the map.

Karen got excited, "Could it have gotten torn when Al's parents dug the cellar years ago?"

Dave and Al looked at each other, "It could have, how many years ago would that have been, Al?" Dave asked.

Al sat back, "Oh, mom's 90 years old and they moved into the house right after they got married. I suppose she was about 16 or 17 years old, so it's been 73 or 74 years ago. Long time!" Al scratched his head and looked at Dave.

Dave thought for a moment. "It could have been torn off then by accident or years before that intentionally. We can only speculate right now."

Al was beside himself. "What do you think we should do?"

Debbie looked at everyone, "It's late and we need to get away from this lodge. Why don't we drive down to the marina and spend the night. In the morning we can go boating. Maybe do a little fishing while we think of what to do, and we could even study the map more. What do you think?"

Al stood up, "That's a good idea. Maybe the crowd that seems to be gathering at Canyon Lake Lodge will have more difficulty spying on us if in fact that is what they were doing.

"If Gene, Marlene, Pastor Gerry and Norma were spying on us I think they are extremely amateur or very cleaver." Debbie said. "Their disguises were poor and their presence obvious. Do you think they intended to be so reckless about it, maybe covering for someone else?"

"Everyone in Mobil Park City knows everyone pretty good so it would be rather stupid to show up and put on a faulty disguise." Karen noted.

"My question is how did they know we were even here. Did you tell anyone where you were going Dave?" questioned Al.

"No, not even our kids." Dave remarked. "Think about this, they were here before we arrived."

Al got up and started pacing, "that's right they were."

"Quit pacing Al, it won't help." Karen urged. "We better quit for the night and get down to the marina." Al left the map with Dave and Debbie. Upon arriving at the marina relief came over all of them and they had a good rest that night.

# CHAPTER 3

*Morning came,* however it brought more distress. Al, Karen, Dave and Debbie were awakened by forest rangers. To their surprise the reason for this was because the clerk at Canyon Lake Lodge was found dead earlier. The Rangers were questioning everyone who was around the Lodge the past twenty-four hours. The rangers reassured them it was routine and that a suspect was in custody. They were told not to leave the area until it had been cleared up incase further questioning was necessary. Dave and Al assured them they would not leave but wanted to go boating for the day. The rangers agreed they could go and left.

"Who do you think killed her?" Karen asked hysterically.

Al put his arm around Karen, "Don't worry it probably has nothing to do with us."

Karen became even more intense, "She was listening to our phone call!" Dave told Karen it could have been someone else; we couldn't be sure who was listening. "But she looked suspicious when I looked at her." Karen argued.

"It still doesn't mean she was listening." Al told her. "Do you think Gene and Marlene, or Pastor Gerry and Norma would be capable of murder?"

Dave gave Al a puzzled look, "No, actually I don't. There is some strange turn of events, but I can't imagine anyone in Mobil Park City being crooked or evil. Besides, Pastor Gerry is supposed to be a man of God. Come on let's go fishing." They packed a lunch and took off in Dave's boat. When they got far away from shore and felt safe enough they put out the fishing lines and Dave took out the map. "Something has been puzzling me, look at this mark and notice the landmarks around it. Do you recognize anything on the map?"

Debbie looked at the map, "What are you calling landmarks, this isn't a real map. It's just a grouping of hieroglyphics and other markings."

Al studied the marks on the map and the mark Dave pointed out. "It's close to Mobil Park City?" Al exclaimed. "What do you make of that?"

"I don't know, except if in fact it is near Mobil Park City I think it's just another clue and could lead to the other half of this map." Dave studied the map turning it every once in a while.

Debbie grabbed Dave's hand. "Stop turning the map so much. I think I have an idea." She moved over by Dave and turned the map a half turn. "What do you call it when you have a picture inside another picture and you have to stare right into the middle of it to make the picture pop out."

Karen perked up, "I know, it's called a Hologram!"

Dave looked up and noticed a boat approaching. "That boat is getting rather close. What do you make of it Al?"

"Maybe they're curious?" Al questioned studying the situation. Just then a shot rang out coming from the boat. Debbie gripped the map as Dave grabbed her and hit the deck. Al hit the deck too, but Karen started screaming and jumping up and down hysterically. Al grabbed her arm and jerked her down to the deck of the boat too. "What do you make of that, Dave?" Al screeched.

Dave jumped up and hit the gas, off they went, Al grabbed the poles and started reeling in their lines. Debbie helped by reeling in Dave's line. "I don't think I want to know who they are I just want to get out of here." Dave yelled.

"Look, Dave! They are following us. Can you go faster?" Debbie suggested in excitement.

"I have it throttled all the way now!" Dave yelled. "Find something to throw at them if they get closer!"

Debbie looked at Dave, "You've got to be kidding! Do you want me to thrust my stinky shoe at them? Do you think that will be more lethal than the bullets they are winging at us?" Debbie proclaimed in utter frustration.

Dave was trying to get the most speed out of his boat but he quickly realized that he would have to be tricky instead. "Don't panic, I have a better idea."

Debbie stood up from crouching on the floor. "I hope so, because they are gaining and fast!"

Al began laughing, "I know, we'll just chuck Karen at them, that will slow them down for a second." He stood up and rolled over the seat in the back.

Karen got up, "Oh very funny, Al! How about we just feed you to them."

"Don't get excited, Karen. Al is just trying to find humor in a most peculiar way." Debbie scowled, "You know Al, this isn't the time to crack funnies. They are catching up with us." Just then a shot came from the boat again. Debbie hit the floor grabbing Karen and knocking her down too. "Stay down Karen and crawl back to the cabin. Gather all the towels and blankets you can find. Also the red life jackets." Debbie crawled to the back. The boat was hitting hard on the water as Dave sped toward the marina. Al was crouched at the back of the boat trying to get a good look at who was chasing them. "Can you make out who it is at all?" Debbie asked.

Al bounced hard on the floor of the boat. "No and the ride is making it difficult to want to keep looking."

"Hey Al, I recognize one of the guys on that boat. He was in the lobby when we first got here." Debbie ducked down. "I also saw him somewhere else, but I can't remember where."

Al realized that Dave was slumped over the steering wheel of the boat. Al pointed to Dave; Debbie quickly jumped up and grabbed him. "Dave, he's shot! Al, he's shot!" Debbie lowered him down to the deck of the boat. Al steered the boat into the marina and the other boat backed off. As soon as they had docked Karen took off to find help and Al stayed with Dave and Debbie.

# CHAPTER 4

*Dave was* rushed to the nearest hospital. Debbie, Al, and Karen arrived shortly after the ambulance had arrived. To their relief the gunshot wound was a deep graze that just missed his temple. This would account for Dave passing out; also, he tends to be wimpy at the sight of blood. Dave was treated and released.

At the marina, forest rangers and the feds were waiting impatiently for them to return. The authorities wanted to question Dave, Debbie, AL, and Karen about the shooting incident earlier that day. To their surprise, David was waiting in the Ranger Station as well. "What are you doing here?" Dave and Debbie asked.

David looked concerned, "I heard about the shooting incident and the home office sent me here to get to the bottom of it. "Are you okay, dad?"

Dave hugged David, "Yes, it was just a graze, nothing serious. We have been watched since we arrived though and can't figure out why."

David turned to the Rangers, "Nothing to worry about. I will be taking over from here. I will let you know of my investigation."

The Rangers looked at Dave, Debbie, Al, and Karen, "You have been in too many places of question since you arrived." Ranger Hank turned to David. "Make sure you clear this up quickly. We already have one dead body, we don't want more."

Back at the motor home Dave explained to David what had transpired. Al looked puzzled, "David, are you a fed?"

David smiled, "Not exactly Al. I work undercover and only show authority when it is necessary.

Al paced for a moment, "Do we show him the map Dave?"

Dave looked at David, "Al found a map and called me to meet him here to see it. Since we arrived there have been some rather bizarre incidents. A clerk at Canyon Lake Lodge turned up dead and we think we saw Gene, Marlene, Pastor Gerry, and Norma wearing disguises watching us. Also, Al and Karen had a room at the lodge and someone ransacked it looking for, we believe, this map."

David looked at the map, "You have been busy. I hate to burst your suspicions about Gene and company. They are in Mobil Park City and haven't left. I have an agent watching them as we speak."

"Why do you have an agent watching Gene and company?" Karen asked.

"Actually, there are several agents watching everyone at Mobil Park City." David confessed. He proceeded to explain to them that there were reasons that just couldn't be revealed at this time.

"And we are supposed to buy that?" Al grumbled.

David put his hand on Al's shoulder, "In short, yes, Al. I will tell you as soon as I can, but for now, I can't."

"We showed you our map and told you everything. Doesn't that earn some trust?" Al questioned. David told him yes, but it was bigger than all that, and he couldn't reveal more information because he needed the trust of his agents too. Al struggled, but agreed to be patient and trust David. "Do you mind if we continue to look for the other half of this map and find what it is all about?" asked Al.

David smiled and handed the map back to Al. "Please do, I will try to offer some protection for all of you, but be careful. Someone must know about it and maybe know more than you do. I am interested in the disguised Gene & company. Is there anything else you can tell me about them?"

Al looked at David curiously, "I thought you said Gene, Marlene,

Pastor Gerry and Norma were still in Mobil Park City. Why are you interested in who we saw?" Al curiously questioned.

David smiled, "In do time Al, I'll inform you of everything." Al shook his head but agreed to quit asking questions.

They all agreed to keep in touch, and Dave and Al would keep looking for the other half of the map and whatever was at the end of it.

# CHAPTER 5

*Morning brought* encouragement. Al decided he and Karen would go back to his mother's house and investigate the cellar where Al had found the first half of the map. David left for Mobil Park City to continue his business, and Debbie and Dave took the map and went with him.

Once back home Dave and Debbie felt somewhat safe, but the events that had preceded them were still fresh in their minds. Dave still had a healthy concern for Al and Karen's safety, but kept pushing it back further in his mind.

Debbie went to work. She owned the local library and wanted to look up some information concerning the map. Dave gave the map to her for reference, but instructed her to be very careful and not let anyone see it. Debbie took the map with her. The library seemed rather busy and that was definitely out of the ordinary. On a normal day there might be four to five people strung through the day, and that would be a good day. Today it was full. About three to four people every hour. Debbie kept the map tucked away in her dress pocket and when she looked up information she tried to be discrete about it.

It was amazing, in a days time the whole town of Mobil Park City seemed to be in need of books. As they poured into the library Debbie took interest in what they required and what everyone was looking for in books. She also paid close attention to what was being checked out. The variety wasn't so big. The subjects consisted of Food preparation, hunting, Indian artifacts, and archeology. Glenn checked out the book that really grabbed Debbie's attention. He seemed particularly interested in maps. Treasure maps dated back from the late 1700s to the early 1800s in the area of Mobil Park City to be specific. Debbie smiled at Glenn as he checked out and tried not to draw attention to her suspicions. As soon as Glenn left the building Debbie quickly called Dave. "Hello, Dave can you talk for a second?"

Dave was resting from his wound and was slightly groggy, "Yes but don't say anything that would draw attention to us."

Debbie scowled, "Dave, Glenn just left the library with a book on maps of Mobil Park City area, dated back in the late 1700s to the early 1800s. What do you think?"

"I don't know, come home and we can discuss this. Did you find anything that would help us read our map?" Dave asked.

"Yes I did, I'll be home in a few minutes." Debbie hung up and gathered her things together. Just about that time Donna the founder of the small town scurried in the door. "I'm about to close, Donna."

Donna waved her arm at Debbie, "I'll only be a second, and I know just what I want to get." Donna hurried over to the book shelves collected two books and checked them out. Debbie observed they were on the legalities of treasure finding. Donna smiled and thanked Debbie for staying open and off she went. Puzzled at all the activity concerning the subject of treasure and maps, Debbie once again gathered her things locked the door and hurried home.

Arriving home she discovered that David was there. Debbie hurried in to say hello and found a concerned Dave and David, "What is the problem? You all look like someone died." Debbie was taken back to learn that Al and Karen's motor home was found abandoned in Sequence. "I thought they were going to see Al's mom in Spokmann. What on earth are they doing in Sequence?"

David told Debbie, his mom, to sit down. "Mom, Karen and Al are not in Sequence that we know of. In fact they never made it to

Spokmann to see Al's mom. In short, they are missing."

Debbie looked around the room, "Oh no, do you have any idea what might have happened to them?"

David tried to be positive, "Maybe, but we can't be sure. If they were kidnapped..." Debbie interrupted.

"What do you mean if? Of course they were abducted! They were going to go to Al's mom's house and look for the other half of the map. It has to have something to do with this map!" Debbie was exasperated. "We have to find what this map is all about before something bad happens to Al and Karen or someone else!"

Dave put his hand on Debbie's shoulder, "We will just stay focused and don't panic. Who knows of their disappearance?" Dave questioned David.

David thought for a moment. "I don't know. I'll have to do some investigating to find out more. Don't worry I'll get to the bottom of this. In the mean time, please be careful and stay together." Dave and Debbie assured David that they would work on the map and stay together.

Dave looked at Debbie, "What did you find concerning the map?"

"I'm not sure, I found some history on the area of Mobil Park City from back in the 1700s through the 1800s. When do you think the map was made?" Debbie asked Dave.

Dave scratched his head and thought for a moment. "I think the map was made in 1830. Now we have to figure out who made the map and what it's purpose was."

"Easy, ha! Like finding a needle in a haystack. We just look until we get stuck." Debbie smiled putting the map on the table and got the books out she had brought home. "Why do you think the map was made in 1830?"

Dave pointed to some worn out scratches on the map. "Get a magnifying glass and look closely at this." Debbie retrieved a glass from the desk and studied the scratches. Then she let Dave look.

"You know," Debbie sat down on the chair and looked at Dave. "Donna checked out a book on legalities of treasure discoveries. What do you make of that?"

"Sometimes, I don't really think we need to be troubled or concerned over what everyone around us is doing." Dave looked up at Debbie. "But then again, sometimes we do."

"So...is this one of those times?" Debbie asked.

Dave sat down, "I don't know, it's strange that everyone here in this town is in the library first and checking out books on the subject of treasure in one form or another. Maybe it is one of those times." Dave sighed. "I'm really worried about Al and Karen. What do you make of the scratches I showed you?"

Debbie looked at the scratches through the magnifier again. "It doesn't look like anything. If this map was made by an Indian there wouldn't be a date on it. So if these scratches are a date, then who made the map?" Debbie sat down and looked at Dave. "Carol told me when she was checking out a book on artifacts, that Glenn was calling a town meeting on Friday. Have you heard?" Debbie glanced up at Dave.

"No I was sleeping all day until you called." Dave got up and retrieved a glass of water. "Is it a regular meeting or a special meeting?"

"I think it's a special meeting, we just had our regular monthly meeting last Tuesday." Debbie stated. Dave was pouring over a book Debbie had brought home. "What did you find that's so interesting?" Debbie noted.

"I'm not sure, could be nothing." Dave reached over and picked up the map. "Look at this, Debbie. I think this mark and the one in the book are exactly alike. What do you make of it?" Dave put the book and the map on the table as Debbie leaned over to look.

"They appear to be alright, maybe this is a break through. By the way Mobil Park City didn't exist until fifteen years ago." Debbie got a pencil and paper to write on. They studied the book and the map most of the night until they were exhausted. Dave collected everything he thought might be pertinent to the map and looked for a safe place to hide it. "Do you think it's all that important to hide the research materials?" Debbie questioned.

Dave thought for a moment, "Maybe not but I just want to make sure for now. In the morning we can regroup and decide what might be important and what to discard."

# CHAPTER 6

By the time Friday arrived there was no news of Al and Karen. Dave and Debbie were even more concerned. Glenn had in fact called a special town meeting, so they went to see what the fuss was all about. Debbie wondered if it had anything to do with the recent surge of book checkouts.

Glenn is the city planner, and has called special meetings in the past but not when key city officials are out of town or missing. He opened the meeting with Judge Joann, Vic the county attorney, Archie the sheriff, and Bill and Barbara the mayor and first lady as the city council. Usually the city engineer is present and a part of the city council as well, however, since he and his wife had disappeared it was no wonder they weren't there. Almost everyone was present, so it was a good turnout for the meeting. Upon opening the meeting, it was quite evident that no one there had any idea Al and Karen were missing. David was quick to say Al and Karen were still visiting Al's mom in Spokmann.

"Why didn't David tell everyone Al and Karen were abducted?" Debbie whispered to Dave.

Dave told Debbie to be still and they would find out soon enough.

Glenn's purpose for the meeting was soon revealed to everyone. He wanted to expand the city limits and needed a citizen vote to do it. He also revealed what the books were all about when he informed them that he had studied the layout of certain artifact areas from the late 1700s to the early 1800s. Exactly what his books were about that he had checked out. Debbie sighed a big sigh. "Why are you relieved?" whispered Dave.

"This is all about expanding not treasure." Debbie whispered.

Dave put his arm around Debbie and whispered quietly..."No it isn't, listen carefully." Dave urged. Debbie sat up and paid attention to what was being said.

Glenn said the area was artifact rich and that it would be important to everyone in the town. He was suggesting that they build a museum and place all artifacts in the museum. Debbie looked back at Dave in question. To her it sounded like a good idea. However Dave had something else going on in his mind. Debbie observed everyone's face as Glenn exposed his plan for the town.

When the meeting was over Debbie started to ask Dave a question and was stopped abruptly as they walked out. "Keep it to yourself until we are alone." Dave whispered hurrying out the door. All around them they could hear the positive attitudes of everyone.

Once home Dave opened up. "I don't think this is an artifact area neither is the close proximity of this town."

Debbie looked puzzled, "How do you know?"

"Because if it were, people would have been finding artifacts all along." Dave was discouraged. "Do you think Glenn has anything to do with Al and Karen's disappearance?" Dave asked.

Debbie hugged Dave, "No, I don't. Granted he plans everything right down to what underwear he's going to wear and why, but no I don't think he's mean or crocked." Debbie stared at the books lying on the table. "Dave, something is different. Look, the books aren't like we left them." In a panic, she started looking around the house, "Someone has been in our house!"

Dave looked around and noticed things were different too. "What did you do with the map?"

"I have it on me. I had it all the time." Debbie looked anxious. "What does this have to do with our map? Al just found it and he had to go to Spokmann to do that accidentally." Debbie started examining what might have been studied on the table. "Let's call David. Maybe he can examine this place and figure out what the intruder was looking for, besides the map."

Dave looked startled at Debbie, "Why do you think someone was looking for more than the map?"

Debbie pointed out the books on the table. "Why would someone re-arrange the books like that if they weren't looking for something other than a map?" Dave sat down at the table. "Don't touch anything Dave. I want to examine the situation."

"Me too." Dave said in heavy thought.

Debbie went to the phone and called David to see if he would come over and study the situation. Upon returning, she noticed a small object on the floor under the table. Walking to the table she leaned over and picked it up. To her surprise, it was a compass, a very old compass. "Look Dave," Debbie handed the compass to Dave. The doorbell rang and Debbie left to answer the door. It was David, "Thank you for hurrying over. I just found an antique compass under the table. Whoever was here must have dropped it.

David followed Debbie into the dinning room. "Hi, dad." David glanced around the room. "Mom said she found a compass."

Dave handed the compass to David. "What do you make of it?"

David examined it with great interest, "Where did you find it?" Debbie explained she found it under the table, and pointed to the approximate spot where it was laying. David handed the compass to Debbie, then preceded to examine every inch of the room. Dave asked if he could help so David shared with him what he was looking for.

Debbie watched David and Dave, "What are you..." David interrupted her with shhhhhhh! Debbie motioned to David to come over to her. There was something in the compass. David frowned, took some tweezers out of his pocket and removed a small object out of the compass. It was a bug! "Oh!" huffed Debbie.

"Shhhhhh!" David held his finger up to his lips. Debbie clammed up immediately. David wrote on a piece of paper, he thought there were more bugs around the house. He motioned for them to get some things and come with him to his house.

Once at David's house, they were sort of relieved but scared to talk for fear there were bugs there too. David reassured them he was bug free. "I have a bug blaster security through out my house so we are safe to talk now."

"Well that's a relief!" Debbie exclaimed. "Why did someone put a bug in an antique compass?"

David explained, "The intruder was hoping you would find the compass and keep it to search for whatever the map had at the end of the trail. Whoever left this compass probably was hoping you would take the compass everywhere with you. Then they could hear what you were up to at all times."

"Do you suppose we have alarmed them to the fact you are an agent?" Dave asked.

"No I don't think so. I think that the culprit that left this compass is in fact one of my agents. I didn't want to release this information until I was sure, but we are pretty sure at this point." David explained.

"Don't worry, son, mom and I won't tell a soul. In fact, put it back in the compass and we will be the moles for you. Just tell us what to do and we will do it." Dave urged.

"None of this has a thing to do with anyone here at Mobil Park City does it?" Debbie said.

David sighed, "Yes it does, but I can't tell you why or who it involves. So please don't ask me, okay?" David proceeded to take the bug out of the compass. He placed a magnetic ring around it and told Dave and Debbie that to use them, as a mole wouldn't be a wise decision. The party that planted the bug was already aware they knew someone was listening."

Debbie looked at David, "Oh No! What about the conversation before we realized we were bugged? We mentioned the map and that perhaps someone was looking for more than the map. We also mentioned the meeting and the fact that this was not an artifact area. Now what do we do?" Debbie was upset and gave Dave a frustrated look.

Dave looked at Debbie, "What?"

Debbie was embarrassed, "I mentioned Glenn's underwear. I didn't mean to make such a comment for someone else to hear."

"Don't worry. I don't think it will matter, but perhaps the disappearance of Al and Karen will be the worse thing we've talked about."

Dave shook his head, "nothing is private anymore."

David laughed, "Don't worry, if it's our guy than he already knows you know who I am, and that Karen and Al have disappeared. However, he might not have known about Glenn's underwear. Sorry mom." David couldn't help but chuckle. "First thing we need to do is to get a sweep over to your house so all the other bugs are found and gotten rid of. I'll inform someone I trust and my suspect won't have a clue.

# CHAPTER 7

*Morning came* and Dave and Debbie looked forward to some normal activity in their lives as they started the day. Dave took off to the office and Debbie went by their home and picked up the books she had brought home the night before from the library.

At the library things seemed pretty slow until Glenn showed up. He was returning the books he had checked out. Shortly after he had arrived in came Vic the county attorney and Judge Joann, Donna, Gene and Marlene, Pastor Gerry and Norma, Mayor Bill and Barbara, and most of the rest of the town citizenship. Everyone returning the books they had checked out, except Carol, she never came in. Debbie was surprised they didn't keep the books longer than a day. It seemed that the library had become the local hub for the day. Everyone milling around talking to each other and very relaxed about being there. What happened to going to work, or whatever they usually do in a day's time? Suddenly the library was grand central station at rush hour and no one seemed to be in a rush to leave. Debbie had thought she would have a quiet day at work but instead she was too busy to think.

As the day drew to an end and the townspeople dribbled out the door Debbie was glad to end her day. She approached the door to lock it and Vic the county attorney ran up the stairs and stopped her. "Wait, wait!" he yelled grabbing the doorknob and entering.

Debbie hadn't quite gotten to the door, but was still surprised to see that her day wasn't exactly at an end. "What do you need Vic?" She questioned.

Vic was slightly out of breath because he had run up to the door. "Well," he panted, "I have been looking for Dave and can't find him so I thought he might be here with you."

Debbie's heart quickened, "No he's not with me, I last saw him at home this morning. He was going to work though. Did you look at the office?" Debbie looked worried.

Vic paused for a moment, "I tried there first, and then your home, no one is around." Vic noticed Debbie was getting slightly stressed. He continued, "I also checked to see if he was over at David's home, but no one was there either."

Debbie looked surprised at the fact that David wasn't home. "Did you check to see if he was at Bob and Donna's home or office?" Vic shook his head yes. Puzzled at this Debbie gathered her thoughts quickly, "Well they have to be around here somewhere. What did you want with Dave?" Debbie's curiosity overtook her obvious concern for Dave.

Vic looked around and for one brief moment wasn't sure he wanted to tell her. "I think what I wanted to talk with Dave about could upset you and cause some concern for his safety." Vic started to leave.

Debbie panicked, "Vic, I am already concerned for his safety. Please tell me what is on your mind.... Vic please, tell me!"

Vic paced back and forth for a moment. "I heard some guys talking over at The Red Sparrow. Cindy was waiting on them and over heard their conversation too."

Debbie grabbed Vic's arm, "Cindy was waiting on whom? And heard whose conversation about what?"

Vic paused..."She waited on two guys that arrived in town about a couple weeks ago. Cindy is talking to Gene and Marlene about what she heard. I was sitting in the booth next to them and Cindy handed me a bill with a note on it instead of a real bill. She urged me to go find Dave and David. When I couldn't find them, I thought maybe they were here with you."

Debbie interrupted Vic. "What did you and Cindy hear? Vic, I need to know!"

Vic looked stern, "They said Dave and David were agents and involved in a secret plot that concerned the safety of every citizen in Mobil Park City." Vic looked down at the ground, then back at Debbie. "Do you know if any of that is true?"

Debbie looked stunned, " I can tell you Dave is no agent, and there is no secret plot on his or David's part. Who were these guys you overheard talking in The Red Sparrow?" Debbie asked Vic.

With a slight hesitation, Vic reluctantly delivered all he was knowledgeable about concerning Dave and David. "I don't know the guys. They have been in town for a couple weeks now, and I have seen David with one of them a time or two. I'm not sure why they think Dave and David are agents, and I don't know why they think all of Mobil Park City is in jeopardy." Vic sighed a big sigh. "That's about everything."

Debbie grabbed Vic's arm, "Listen to me carefully, Dave and David are in grave danger. Al and Karen are also in grave danger, and hopefully still alive! We have to get some people together we can trust and work out a plan to help them. I'll be right back." Debbie ran to get her things and returned. After locking the door, Vic and Debbie headed down the road to locate Joann and return to The Red Sparrow Inn.

Vic was shook up from Debbie's information, "Why would Al and Karen be in danger? Aren't they visiting Al's mother?" He panted out of breath as they rushed down the street.

"There's so much you don't know about all this Vic, and I haven't the time to explain it twice. Just trust me and hurry. We must gather as many people as possible and make sure we can trust them. Then I'll explain what I know." Debbie was worried for Dave and David's safety. Many questions rushed through her mind as they hurried along. Where were Dave and David? Who were the guys in the diner? Should she reveal all or just some of the truth?

They reached Vic's house and saw quite a few towns' people there. Debbie stopped abruptly. "What's wrong?" Vic asked, as he stopped looking back at Debbie.

Debbie looked at Vic in a panic, "Why are so many people at your house?"

Vic turned to look at the driveway and yard where many had gathered. "I don't know." He looked puzzled. "What do you make of it?

Debbie studied the gathering. "Look Vic, over by the porch stairs. Are those the two guys you saw in The Red Sparrow?"

Studying the two men Debbie had pointed out, Vic realized it was the two from the Inn. "Do you think those two men are stirring up some trouble?" Vic noticed Joann; she was standing on the porch by the front door. He waved at her and managed to get her attention.

Debbie looked at Vic and jumped behind a tree. "What are you doing?" She yelled in a whisper. "Don't draw attention to us!"

Vic told Debbie not to worry. Then he used hand signals to get Joann to go around back. He slipped behind a tree too. "We can meet her behind the house and find out what is going on." Vic explained to Debbie.

"Okay" Debbie agreed. "Just don't let the two men see us. They may know where Dave and David are. I think they're up to no good."

Vic and Debbie made their way to the back of the house where Joann was waiting.

Joann spotted them in the bushes and waved them over. "What are you doing sneaking around here, and why didn't you just come home normal?"

"Shhhh" Vic quieted Joann. "The two men in front by the porch stairs, what do they want here?

Joann looked at Vic like he had lost his senses. "They wanted a town meeting. The tall one Smyth, he said it was an emergency, we were all in danger."

Debbie was upset. "Someone's in danger alright but no one here. We need to go to a private place so no one knows we are here." Debbie paced nervously, "Don't tell anyone we are here. My guess is they will tell you Dave and David are plotting against the town putting everyone in danger. That they, the two men, are agents working to break a ring of double agents run by Dave and David. Actually Dave isn't an agent at all. I do know that the two men are in fact working as agents, but up to something illegal. They were being investigated by real agents." Debbie held up her hand. "I know it all sounds too bizarre. Believe me, unless we find Dave and David, I'm not sure we'll ever know what is really going on. And to think this crazy mess started when Al and Karen found that stupid map!"

Joann and Vic looked startled. "What map?" They both replied in shock.

Debbie stood there desperate, "Look, I'll tell you everything, but first please get us somewhere safe and remotely sound proof!"

Joann told Vic to go into a back room and she would stay with the crowd until the two men had said what they had come to say. "No promises, but I'll try to keep everyone settled down and sane for as long as I can. When it's over I'll get some of the people we can trust gathered up, and we'll have our own meeting." Joann hurried back to the front yard.

Vic and Debbie retreated to a back room, but stayed where they could hear what was going on in the front yard. Sure enough, the two men Smyth and Wessin worked the crowd. The story was Dave and David were double agents who had been working the town for several years. Strangely enough the story they fed the towns people was so bizarre, that the people shook their heads at the whole idea. Half of them left and went home laughing at such a story. One even made the comment that the guys should write a story it might make a good book. When the evening drew to a close and most everyone had left, the two men thanked Joann for her help. Then reassured her that they would work hard to protect the town and people, even if they didn't believe the information. Joann thanked them and the two men left.

Cindy was disturbed by the meeting and stayed to talk to Joann. She wasn't alone. Harley, Carol, Gene, Marlene, Pastor Gerry, Norma, Donna, Bob, Glenn, Augie, Phyllis, Bill and Barb were also disturbed by the tall tale and stayed to talk to Joann about it.

Glenn noticed Vic hadn't been at the meeting. "Where is Vic, Joann? Isn't he usually home by now?"

Joann looked around, "Yes, he's home." She replied. "Quietly go to the back room and take them with you." Joann motioned for Glenn to take the group with him. Glenn mingled and told everyone to go to the back room quietly. After the small group of concerned citizens slowly retreated to the back room, Joann made sure everyone else had left. Then she locked the door.

Once in the back room, everyone started asking Debbie what the story was concerning Dave and David. Debbie studied all of their faces. "I need to know I can trust everyone here."

They all looked around at each other. Harley spoke up, "Of course you can trust us. We've been friends for years. Always watching each other's backs. Why all the suspicion now?"

Debbie looked serious at each and every one of them. "After what Smyth and Wessin just told you, are you not suspicious of Dave and David?"

Harley giggled while others laughed, "No, we know Dave and David better than that."

Carol added, "And a lot longer than we have known Agents Smyth and Wessin.

Debbie admitted she was frustrated with the two agents and their story. "However," she explained, "the truth is almost as bizarre as their story." Debbie reluctantly told all she knew. "In short, the story is; Dave and I had met Karen and Al at Canyon Lake Lodge because Al had found an old map in his mother's cellar. There were some old Indian markings on it, and they wanted to know if we knew what they meant. The plot thickens when the Canyon Lake Lodge clerk, who they thought listened in on the phone conversation, was murdered. We thought we saw Gene, Marlene, Pastor Gerry and Norma disguised at the Lodge.

Sorry guys, nothing personal. However, David was interested in that bit of information." Debbie looked stern at Gene, Marlene, Pastor Gerry and Norma. " Can I trust you, or are you a part of all this mess?" She questioned them.

They all looked stunned, Pastor Gerry spoke up. "No we are not a part of this mess. We had no idea Al and Karen had found a map." He was shook by the information and the accusation.

Gene was equally surprised. "Does David actually think we are capable of murder? We have been friends with everyone here including Al and Karen for years. How could you possibly suspect us?" Gene was concerned.

Debbie looked at all of them. "There's more; Dave, Al, Karen and I went boating to examine the map. We were accosted by another boat. Bullets started flying and the race to the marina was on. Dave was shot, but it was just a graze, and David revealed he was an agent working on a case that involved Mobil Park City. That's when David informed us that Gene, Marlene, Pastor Gerry and Norma couldn't have been at the Lodge because they never left town. Dave discovered that there must be another half to the map.

After that we returned home while Karen and Al went back to his mothers to look for what we believed to be the other half of the map. A few days later David told us that Al and Karen disappeared in Sequence, or so he assumed because their motor home was found abandoned there. We don't know what happened to them. Al's mom told David they never returned after they left the first time."

Everyone sat and looked at Debbie like she was as good a storyteller as the two strangers who tried to stir them up that night. Debbie looked around the room. "I hate to say it but we were suspicious of everyone here. Especially when Glenn called an emergency meeting about artifacts, and everyone was checking out books on maps, artifacts and the city. What was I to think?" Debbie was frustrated. "Now Dave and David are missing, and somewhere in all this mess, David told me he suspected one of his agents of some wrong doings. He wasn't specific."

Glenn scratched his head, "Wait a minute. You think I'm mixed up in this mess because I called a special meeting?" Glenn stood up, "I thought you knew me! Why didn't you ask me? Al and I have been friends, I certainly wouldn't put his life in jeopardy."

"Okay Glenn, I'm sorry." Debbie apologized. "David told me not to trust anyone. Now look, I have to trust you. I would like to know who told you this town was artifacts rich? Debbie asked Glenn. Everyone looked at Glenn.

Glenn looked around at everyone. "The two guys, Smyth and Wessin. What can I say, they made it believable!" Glenn hung his head and shuffled his feet.

Bill stood up, "As mayor of this town I think we need to get organized and try to find out what is actually going on. Don't worry Glenn it could happen to anyone. Now let's find Dave and David, the trail couldn't be too cold yet. Maybe we'll find Karen and Al too. I'll call Sheriff Archie and we'll get started right now."

Everyone agreed that they should help. Bill, Barb, Donna and Norma were to be the base team. It was also agreed that no one should be alone. They all were to travel in groups of three or four until the whole situation was cleared up.

They decided to break up into small groups. Pastor Gerry, Gene and Marlene made up group1. Vic, Joann, and Bob made group 2. Debbie, Cindy, and Glenn made up group 3. Harley, Carol, Dan and Lucille, group 4. All were to report to the base team with their group numbers.

Bill decided the best place to start would be when and where Dave and David were last seen. Not an easy task.

Glenn decided to work on a spreadsheet with the times and places they were seen. Everyone sat down to discuss when and where Dave and David were seen that day. Debbie had been with them that morning at David's house just before Dave left for the office and she left for the library. The time was 7:30 AM. Shortly after she arrived at the Library, maybe 8:10 AM, Dave called and told her they were going to The Red Sparrow for coffee. David had to meet with two of his agents. Glenn put the times and places on his spreadsheet.

Pastor Gerry and Gene remembered they had seen them at The Red Sparrow that morning too. Cindy said she waited on Dave and David and they arrived about 8:20 AM. Gene and Pastor Gerry remembered arriving at the Inn about 9:30 AM. Glenn sighed, "Does anyone remember if they talked to someone or when they left?"

Cindy thought for a moment. "Yes, they talked to the two guys Smyth and Wessin. Not long though, maybe five minutes. Then they left around 9:50 AM.

"When did Agents Smyth and Wessin leave?" Glenn asked.

"About 10:30 AM, I believe is when they left." Cindy noted.

Vic remembered seeing Dave and David at the hardware store around 11:00AM. Donna saw Dave and David at the Post Office at 2:12 PM or close to that. Glenn asked what they were doing, what they bought, and so forth. They were talking to Harley at the Hardware store and didn't buy anything. Harley said it was just chitchat, nothing that would help in locating them. At the Post Office they were just mailing letters. Finally it was narrowed down to the last place they were seen. It was at 4:00 PM and they had waved at Carol as they were leaving town going north.

Debbie thought for a minute. "Why would they be leaving town? I have to go home and check the answer machine. Maybe they tried to call me at home." Debbie and the rest of group 3, slipped out the back door so they wouldn't be seen and made their way to her house. Upon arriving they were careful not to be seen by anyone. Debbie, Cindy, and Glenn slipped through the dark shadows to the back. Debbie hesitated, "Stop" she whispered. "The door is open."

Glenn examined the door, "It's been forced open." Glenn quietly listened to see if he could hear anything. "You wouldn't happen to have a flashlight would you?" Glenn jokingly asked Debbie. She handed a flashlight to Glenn. "What are you doing with a flashlight?" Glenn looked shocked.

"Are you kidding? With what's been going on I wouldn't be caught without it." Debbie whispered. "Let's go in and check it out."

Glenn grabbed Debbie's arm, "What if someone is in there?"

Debbie patted his arm, "We have the element of surprise it's okay."

Cindy stopped Debbie, "Not if they know we are here and about to enter."

"It's my house guys, I need to go in." Said Debbie. "Stay here, if I'm not back in a couple minutes go for help."

"We are supposed to stay together, number one rule," Cindy argued.

"We all go in and watch each others backs. Let's go." Glenn led the way. "Where is your answer machine?" whispered Glenn.

"Over here!" Debbie answered as quietly as she could.

Glenn flashed the light around the room. "It's clear, I don't see anyone."

Debbie listened to the messages; there were two. One message was from Cindy and the other from Dave. He and David were going to Trepid Falls and would be back in the morning. That would explain them leaving town going north but not why they went to Trepid Falls. Debbie erased the messages.

Glenn found his way over to the answer machine, Debbie, and Cindy. "Did anyone else listen to the messages?"

"No I don't think so the message light was blinking and if you listen to the messages it quits blinking." Debbie replied. "It doesn't mean the guys weren't followed though." Debbie walked over to the light switch and turned the lights on.

Glenn jumped and ran over to turn off the lights. "What are you doing? What if someone is watching and waiting for you to come home? Someone broke into your home and nothing is solved yet." Glenn shook his head. "Dave and David may or may not be safe. We still need to be on this until we know."

Debbie looked around the dark room. "Your right, I'm sorry I wasn't thinking. We still don't know who broke in. However we have our suspicions. Maybe Sheriff Archie would come over tomorrow and see if there are fingerprints."

"We better check in, base team may be getting worried." Glenn suggested. They very carefully closed the back door and put some obstacles in front of it so they could tell if someone returns. Then they returned to Joann's house. Not knowing what else they could accomplish that night, everyone decided it might be wise to stay together for safety reasons. All the women retired into the den and the men stayed in the living room.

Debbie tossed and turned worrying about Dave and David. Cindy moved over to talk quietly with Debbie. "Are you asleep?" Asked Cindy.

"No, I'm worried. I haven't heard from Dave or David. Not to mention the loud snoring, moaning and groaning coming out of the living room." Debbie replied anxiously.

Cindy giggled, "They are loud aren't they." Debbie shook her head and then realized it was dark and Cindy couldn't see her head nod.

"Yes, Shh listen, somebody is talking in their sleep." Debbie whispered. Cindy and Debbie listened and were soon joined by Joann, Marlene, Donna, Carol, Lucille and the rest. It began to get pretty entertaining.

Joann giggled, "let's go see who is dreaming out loud." She motioned for the rest of the ladies to follow her into the living room.

# CHAPTER 8

*Glenn woke* up rubbing his eyes. It must have been about three o'clock in the morning, he wasn't sure. There was a fog all about the room, a window was open and the curtains were fluttering around the silhouette of a sleek figure in the dark bathed in the moonlight. Glenn rubbed his eyes again. Who was there? "Who are you?" He felt groggy, like a heavy drug kept him from moving. The figure floated toward him, Glenn was stunned at the beauty she possessed. "Ohhhhhhhh! He sighed.

"Shh" she placed her finger to his lips.

Once again Glenn tried to speak, "Whoooo, Whooo" He became numb at the touch of her soft skin.

"Shh," she said as she slowly brushed his lips with hers.

"Ohhhhhhhh! Ohhhhhhh!" Glenn slid his hands gently across her bareback. "Mmmmmmm," He groaned as their lips interlocked in a strong embrace. Glenn began to sweat as her moist body pressed against him. "More, ohhhh, more." He encouraged as he grabbed her luscious bare body and they plummeted to the floor.

The lights came on and Glenn stood up startled. "Who turned on the…" As he stood up and turned around, everyone was standing there looking at him. In one surprised look, Glenn scrambled to hide a nude woman that wasn't there. In shock, Glenn stammered "What?" then gathered himself together and plopped down on the sofa where he had been sleeping.

Joann was smiling, as was everyone who had heard and watched the fiasco. "Glenn, was it a good dream?" Joann giggled.

Many of the guys started laughing and chimed in, "It must have been good, look at him blush!"

Debbie and Cindy laughed and told Glenn he needed to avoid sleepovers if he were to dream so loudly in the future. Glenn was upset to say the least. "Why can't all of you refrain from eves dropping?" A guy can't even have a delicious dream without interference.

"Hold it Glenn, you can't go back to sleep. It's time to get to work on finding Dave and David." Vic announced.

Glenn got upset. "No way man, I'm really needing to get back to my dream."

Debbie snatched Glenn's blanket. "Not now champ, there are lives at stake and I mean real ones. So hop to it and let's get going."

Cindy clapped her hands three times and chimed in, "Yep, let's get going."

"Man, a guy doesn't get any rest around here." Glenn complained as he followed everyone out the door.

Vic and Joann had everything organized and began lining everyone out for the day. They were supposed to stay in groups of three or better yet, groups of at least six. Once everyone was in a group, they began to search for clues of the missing men, Dave and David. All were told to avoid Smyth and Wessin, the two strangers who tried to get everyone worked up. Cindy hurried off to work, as did everyone who needed to be in their normal place so they didn't draw attention to the fact that they were checking out Smyth and Wessin. Debbie headed for home accompanied by Vic, Joann, Glenn, and Sheriff Archie. They were going to check her house for fingerprints. Debbie was hoping Dave and David had returned home as their message had indicated. A message would be nice too if they weren't home yet, she thought.

## CHAPTER 9

*Debbie entered* her home, seeing the mess in the daylight from the night before convinced her she needed to be careful. She was no doubt distressed over Dave and David missing and now someone had violated their home. "Don't touch a thing," exclaimed Sheriff Archie. "Let me get my guys in here to sweep it for evidence."

"Archie, I would like to check the answer machine. Is it okay?" Debbie inquired.

Archie looked up from his cell phone, "No not yet, I want to sweep the answer machine for fingerprints." Archie started looking around.

Debbie was frustrated at the mess left by the intruders and the lack of communication with Dave and David. Joann noticed the tension, "Don't worry Debbie. Dave and David are together and very resourceful, I'm sure they are okay. Did you check your cell phone for messages?"

"Oh!" exclaimed Debbie. "In all this mess I didn't think about my cell phone. I left it in the den." Debbie took off to find her cell phone.

The deputies arrived in a short time and began to sweep the house for clues. Debbie found her cell phone and discovered that Dave had left her another message. After listening to Dave's message she disappeared out the back door. Sheriff Archie looked around, "Where did Debbie go?"

Joann replied, "She went to the den to get her cell phone."

"No," Sheriff Archie argued. "She came back talking on her cell phone. I looked down at some evidence and when I looked up she was gone."

Vic looked around, "Wasn't she just listening to messages on her cell phone?"

Joann went out the front of the house to see if Debbie had gone outside. Sure enough Debbie was backing out of the drive. Joann waved her hands in the air to stop her. "Wait!" yelled Joann.

Debbie stopped and rolled down the window, "I don't have time to explain, Joann, I just have to go, now!"

Joann approached the car and opened the door. "Where do you think you have to go?"

Debbie was anxious, "I am going to Trepid Falls."

Joann was puzzled. "Not alone, Debbie, you know we decided to stick together."

Debbie became frustrated, "I know, but sometimes plans change, and I have no choice but to go."

Joann entered the car and closed the door. "Okay, then let's go together. At least you won't be alone."

Debbie sped away before anyone else could stop them. "Joann, I really don't think you should come with me. I don't know what I will find at the falls and I don't want you to get hurt."

Joann grabbed the dash as Debbie flew around the corner-leaving town. "I don't think what we find will be as deadly as your driving! Slow down and tell me why you think you need to go to Trepid Falls."

"I can't slow down, I feel an urgency to get there." Debbie was agitated. "Won't Vic wonder what happened when he can't find you?"

Joann smiled, "you are avoiding my question! What's the hurry and why do you have to go at all!"

"Who's avoiding whose question?" Debbie asked. "Since you are with me I guess I might as well tell you. The message on my cell phone was a coded message. Dave and I worked out a code so we could leave a message for each other in case of emergency or we needed to meet and didn't want anyone to know who or where. To be honest with you, I can't tell you what the message was, just that I had to go."

Joann smiled, "Don't worry so much, Dave and David are okay and I have a feeling Al and Karen are too. Vic will worry so I'll call him when you think it will be safe. Will that work for you?"

Relieved Debbie said yes. It took about two hours to get to Trepid Falls. Debbie slowly drove toward the falls and then took a narrow not so well traveled road to the right that circled around through some trees. No one was in sight.

It was about three o'clock in the afternoon and the shadows were getting rather dark by now. "These trees are rather thick." Joann mentioned. "Do you see anyone around here?"

"No." Debbie replied, "and let's hope we don't see anyone."

Joann was puzzled, "Why don't you want to find Dave and David?"

Debbie stopped the car and turned it off. "I do but they aren't here. My message was to check out something here and meet them somewhere else."

"Are you going to keep me in the dark or tell me what's going on?" Joann asked rather concerned.

"Yes, I'm going to tell you what's going on. Get out of the car and come with me. I'll tell you on the way." Debbie hoped no one was in the vicinity of the falls. Joann got out of the car with Debbie. "We have to be quiet incase somebody is around." Joann followed Debbie through the thick bushes and trees. Slowly they made their way to the pool of trepid falls. Debbie stopped at the edge of the thick brush and trees. "Shh," whispered Debbie. "Someone is coming." Debbie ducked down in the brushes. Joann just stood there. "Psst!" Debbie reached up and grabbed Joann's arm. "Get down!"

Joann ducked behind the bushes with Debbie. "Are you going to tell me what we are after and why you think you needed to come all the way out here?"

"Shh!" Debbie looked at Joann, and then pointed at two men coming down a trail from off the top of the falls. "Quiet, they can't even suspect we are here. We'll talk when they are gone, I promise!" whispered Debbie.

The two men followed the trail down to the pool and stood there looking around. Debbie realized they weren't someone she had seen before. About that time Joann tugged on Debbie's sleeve and pointed in back of them. They both ducked down clear to the ground. About ten feet from where they were hiding someone else was approaching. "Did you bring it?" Asked one of the men.

A familiar voice replied, "No I couldn't find it." At that moment Debbie gave Joann a startled look. The man with the familiar voice walked over to the other men. Debbie and Joann got a fair look at him. As he spoke Debbie became anxious. "I think she has the map on her, it wasn't in her house. I have lost track of her and Joann."

One of the other guys asked how in the world he could loose Debbie and Joann. "I thought everyone was staying together in groups so no one else disappears."

"They are, but this morning when we were at her house investigating I turned my back for a moment and she was gone. Shortly after that Joann left. It was out of character for both of them. Debbie and Joann always tell someone where they are going. Joann didn't even tell Vic, now that's really strange. I finished up the investigation at Debbie's house. Vic told me he and Glenn were going to go look for the women. I knew I needed to meet with you so I waited till I could leave and not be noticed, then I left to come here."

Debbie peaked up through the grass; there she saw Sheriff Archie and another guy with the two by the pool. The man who was with the Sheriff turned, he looked somewhat familiar to Debbie. She taxed her memory trying to remember where she had seen him before. Suddenly it hit her; she had seen the man when Dave and her had met with Al and Karen at Canyon Lake Lodge. Debbie remembered seeing him in the lobby sitting on a couch watching them. Of course she thought a sheriff knows what most people are up to in a small community like Mobil Park City. Why did Sheriff Archie want to harm us, or Al, Karen, David and Dave? What would make him put everything on the line? Debbie buried her head down in the grass. Joann poked Debbie. When she looked up at her Joann pointed to the group of men. They were leaving. Joann and Debbie sunk down as far as they could in hopes Sheriff Archie and his companion would not detect them as they left. The other two left by another path. When Debbie and Joann couldn't hear them any more they slowly and carefully raised up to see if it was clear.

"Do you see them anymore?" Whispered Joann.

Debbie looked around and studied the paths the four men took. "No I don't think so. We have to be careful; they want the map I have been carrying. That's why they were in my house and why Al and Karen are missing.

Joann looked concerned. "Do you think Dave and David are safe?"

Debbie looked at Joann and smiled, "I can guarantee they are safe. Come on lets get what we came for and get out of here."

Joann was all for getting out of there. "What did we come for?"

Debbie took off her shoes and socks and proceeded to wade into the pool. "We came for the key to our map. Keep watch and if anyone comes hide in the bushes but farther from the path. I'll be careful when I come back up to the surface."

Joann looked surprised, "Are you going to swim somewhere?"

Debbie turned back to her, "Yes, I am going to dive down to a cave and retrieve the key. Don't look so worried; I am going to be okay. Just watch for me incase those guys or Sheriff Archie come back. And be quiet." Debbie dove down and entered an underwater cave that came up on the other side of the falls. Years ago they had discovered the cave and spent some great times there.

Joann stepped back into the tall bushes to wait and watch. It had been quite awhile and Debbie wasn't back. Joann was afraid it might get dark before she returned safe and sound. In the twilight it was quiet and should have been peaceful, but Joann was getting more and more concerned. From out of the darkness Joann heard a whisper, "Joann, where are you?"

Joann strained to see in the darkness, "I'm right here. Did you get the key?"

Debbie approached her, "Yes, I did." She whispered. Sorry it took so long. I didn't think finding it would be so complicated."

Joann looked at Debbie, "Well where is it and what does it look like?"

Debbie held up a large rather muddy looking object. "This is it." She said with a smile.

Joann was confused, "You said you were going to get a key not a slimy hunk of mud. How can this be the key?"

Debbie was cold and anxious to get to the car and depart from the falls. "In time, Joann we will all see. Right now we need to get out of here and quick."

"Okay." Joann agreed. The trail was hard to see in the darkness. Joann led the way as they quietly and carefully made their way back to the car. Just short of the area where they had left the car, Joann stopped abruptly.

"What is it Joann?" Debbie whispered.

Joann crouched down, "I'm not sure, did you hear anything that seemed unnatural?" Debbie listened quietly.

After a brief moment Debbie touched Joann's arm and leaned over to whisper. "I did hear something." The two women perched in some tall grass just off the path. It was so dark that they couldn't see much of anything.

Joann tugged at Debbie's sleeve, "Look," she whispered. "What do you think?"

Debbie studied the general direction of where she thought her car might be. Sure enough there was a tiny glowing amber but not constant. About every so many seconds the amber would glow again. Debbie sniffed the air. "It's someone smoking." Debbie whispered to Joann. "Whoever it is might not be alone. Take my keys and I will try to draw them away from the car. Be careful, I may not be able to draw everyone away from the car. So if you make it to the car and in it, lock the doors and drive like crazy to get out of here. I'll meet you down where the stream crosses the road. If I'm not there when you arrive you have to keep going. Don't stop for anyone unless it's me. Oh maybe not, If I'm not alone I won't be so anxious to stop you or get into the car. So pay attention, okay!" Debbie was nervous but knew it was their only chance to get out of there in the dark.

Joann grabbed Debbie's arm as she proceeded to leave. "Stop, don't you have a better plan? What if I get caught or worst yet, what if you get caught? And with the map and key!" Joann was nervous.

Debbie thought for a moment, "No worries, let out a yell as loud as you can. I'll know that you are caught and I'll figure out another plan.

Oh, here take the key but don't let it fall into the wrong hands. Throw it into the tall grass if you get caught. We'll get it later."

Joann insisted they make an alternative plan right then so they weren't flying by the seat of their pants. Debbie told her that it was a fly by the seat of their pants situation and the main plan was for both of them to escape from this place and meet Dave. What ever it would take, they would improvise to ensure their success. With that Debbie slipped out into the darkness. Joann watched for her signal to descend to the parked car. In her mind, she was figuring out how she could be undetected and accomplish her task without being apprehended.

Suddenly Joann was shook by a loud noise. It was like trees crashing down on each other. Some car lights came on and three men rushed to get into a truck. The truck was parked near Debbie's car. About that time Debbie was caught in the headlights. She wheeled around and started running down the road. Joann took off and slipped and slid down the embankment trying to be careful not to be noticed or caught by anyone who might have been left behind to watch the car. Once she was down the embankment she stopped. It was dark once again, but the stillness was disrupted by the noise of the truck chasing Debbie. Joann slowly crept out toward the car stopping once in awhile to survey the area. She finally made it to the car and inside. Nervously she started the car and took off down the road toward the highway. "Please," she begged, "let Debbie be at the crossing." Joann drove like a crazy woman not knowing what she might encounter. There it was, the crossing, but there was no sign of Debbie. She slowed down and crossed slowly cracking her window incase Debbie yelled to her. Nothing, Joann kept driving as Debbie had instructed her. About one mile down the road, Debbie came flying out of the bushes just ahead. Joann slammed on her breaks as Debbie dashed over to the car. About that time the truck flew out of the bushes. Joann panicked; Debbie grabbed the door handle and opened the door just as Joann unlocked the doors. "Go, Go," Debbie yelled. Joann floored the gas pedal and off they flew. The truck ended up in a barrel ditch but managed to get out quickly enough to come up hot on their heels. "Can't you go faster?" Debbie yelled.

Joann was frustrated, "no, I already have it floored and there's no more speed coming out of this little car."

Debbie thought for a minute, "Do you know these back roads at all?"

Joann was driving for all she was worth. "No I don't know these roads and I don't even know this road. I am just driving with the force. Suppose you enlighten me on where to go."

Debbie put her hand on Joann's shoulder, "We need to trade places."

"You've got to be kidding!" Joann was not only frustrated but also shocked at such a suggestion. "We can't stop now they will catch us."

"No worries, Joann." Debbie encouraged. "I have an idea. I'll just drop my seat back as far as it will go and climb in the back seat. You keep your feet on the gas and move over to my seat. I'll take the wheel and as soon as you are moved into the passenger seat, keeping you're left foot over on the gas. I'll climb into the seat and take over the driving." Debbie promptly dropped her seat back.

Joann looked over at Debbie. "You've got to be kidding! Women like us don't change seats while driving fast down a bumpy dirt road, being chased by bad guys in a compact car! It's impossible to do."

Debbie was already climbing into the back seat. "No, Joann it's not impossible when your life depends on it. Now move over and I'll take the wheel." Joann gave up the wheel and the car was swerving all over the road. They both started giggling so hard, they couldn't see the road let alone switch places. Finally the switch was successful. Debbie floored the tiny car into gear and they flew down the road. "I'll bet you will think twice before you follow me again."

Joann laughed, "No, I like to think I have been some help and your adventures are not only intense, but loaded with fun. Now how do we ditch these guys?"

Debbie looked in her rearview mirror. "Maybe we hurry to the highway and go the opposite way we want to go throwing them off from our trail."

Joann thought for a moment, "They will be waiting for us to return to town and Sheriff Archie will be there to take the map from you. After that what will happen to Al and Karen, or Dave and David for that matter?"

"Maybe they'll slow down if they think we are going back to town.

We could loose sight of them and turn off before they catch up with us. There's a road that circles around and goes back to the highway. They'll think we fell into Sheriff Archie's hands. What do you think?" Debbie looked over at Joann. "Look the highway is just up ahead."

Joann looked behind them, "It's worth a try. But the road can be seen from the highway. They will see our lights."

Debbie smiled, "No they won't we will turn them off and creep past them. As soon as they are out of sight we'll turn the lights back on and go ninety until we have plenty of space between us."

"It's dark out here, what if we can't see the road?" Joann was concerned but knew they had to try. "Okay, let's do it."

Debbie and Joann made it to the highway and headed back to town. "Be on the lookout for anything unusual. Like a roadblock or something of the like." Debbie suggested.

Joann gripped the dash, "You think they will call ahead?"

Debbie looked once again in her rearview mirror. "Yes I do."

Joann got upset, "Why didn't you say that when we were formulating our plan?"

Debbie was quiet for a moment, "I just thought of it that's why. There is another road we could take. Look they are backing off from us."

Joann looked behind them at the truck; sure enough the truck had backed off considerably. "Just around this corner and down a small hill there's a gulch. If we make it pull into it quickly."

Debbie was surprised, "Joann, I thought you didn't know the area."

Joann smiled, "I do, but cat and mouse hasn't been my game until now and I think we won't make it to the road you were thinking of. For that matter we may not make it to the gulch. I suggest we move with caution, so slow down. Just as you get to the corner turn your lights off. That way the guys in the truck following will think we went around the corner and if there is someone around the corner they might not see us."

Debbie was surprised. "You are a crafty woman after all Joann. Where have you been hiding all your cleverness?" Debbie giggled as she approached the corner she slowed down and hit her lights at just the appropriate moment. "What should I do now?" She questioned Joann.

Joann was looking behind them to see if they lost sight of the truck. No such luck, it was still coming but slower than before. "Go around the corner and slowly down the hill to the gulch. If you see any vehicles we'll have to leave the road as soon as possible and rule out the gulch."

Debbie proceeded around the corner and all seemed clear. Then down the hill. "Whatever I do, I can't hit the break. If someone is around they will surely see the break lights."

Joann studied the area, "Don't worry once we have come to the gulch if you can get into it without the breaks that's good but if not do it quickly and only once. I'll keep an eye out for the truck."

Debbie geared down as far as she could and slowed to nearly a stop then took the hill. Once she hit the bottom she slammed on the breaks when Joann gave her the okay. Debbie slipped into the gulch and under the brush. She turned the car off and looked back with Joann to see if the truck had passed yet. They waited almost breathless. It seemed like forever before the lights of the truck passed by them. After it went by they both let out a big sigh and jumped out of the car. Running over to the highway to see the tail lights disappear over the hill. "Wow!" Exclaimed Debbie, "that was exhausting."

Joann started back to the car, "we better get turned around as quickly as possible or we will have them on our trail and won't be able to get rid of them."

Debbie agreed. Soon they were back on the highway. With the gas pedal floored, off they flew. "We have to ditch and hide this car for awhile. Do you have any ideas?" Debbie asked Joann.

It was definitely the thing to do but where could they go? They both sat quietly in thought as they sped down the dark desolate highway.

# CHAPTER 10

*Debbie and* Joann drove for about an hour toward the next small town, Heavenly. Debbie remembered some friends that owned a small farm about fifteen miles from the city limits. "Do you think Phyllis and Augie made it home?" Debbie asked Joann.

Joann came out of her deep thoughts, "I didn't even think of them. Are we close to where they live? I haven't been paying attention to where we are."

Debbie checked the area and replied, "Yes the turn off is just up here about ten more miles I think. I hate to put them in jeopardy, but I can't think of anyone else nearby. Do you think they returned home after the meeting?"

"Yes, Phyllis told me they were going home after Smyth and Wessin talked to everyone. If they found out we were in trouble and didn't ask for their help, I think it would upset them. I'm sure they would love to help us." Joann stated. "They may even have some ideas for us."

Debbie turned off the highway towards their farm. Upon approaching the entrance to Augie and Phyllis's place Debbie hesitated. "Something doesn't seem right here, what do you think?"

Joann surveyed the area, "What exactly are you seeing? It looks normal to me." Debbie slowed down as she approached the farmhouse.

"Wait," Joann suggested. "I think you are right, something is wrong. Quick, turn around and get out of here."

Debbie stopped and they surveyed the area. "It appears as though everything is okay, but I'm not sure. I have a strange feeling it isn't. Now I'm worried about Augie and Phyllis."

Joann saw a shadow moving slowly in the dark. "Debbie, someone is here besides Augie and Phyllis. Do you suppose they knew we would come here to see them?"

"Yes, I do." Debbie sat looking around. "Where do you think Augie and Phyllis are?"

Joann looked at Debbie, "should we really care at this moment? We are in trouble and if we don't leave we will be the next to disappear. Oh, and have you forgotten that you now have the key and the map! What are you thinking?" Joann was getting greatly disturbed over Debbie's hesitation.

Debbie looked at Joann and smiled. "No worries, we will spring Augie and Phyllis free from whoever has them and get out of here."

Joann looked at Debbie in a panic, and Joann doesn't usually panic.

"You've got to be kidding! I think you have read to many books sitting around that library. We are not spies, or agents, or guys that go rushing in to save the day. We are two untrained women trying to save ourselves." Joann gasped, "What are you thinking?"

Debbie looked sternly at Joann, "Get a grip, Joann. If I were in their shoes, I would want someone to try and get me out of there. Don't worry; I may have a plan that just might work. We're smart and together we can do it. What do you say?"

Joann looked at Debbie, "We better think and talk faster because we are about to be surrounded." Debbie floored the gas pedal and off they flew, leaving a cloud of dust. "What are you doing? Please enlighten me quick!"

Debbie was driving like a wild woman stirring up as much dust as possible. "I'm creating a cloud for cover. When I stop, I hope I'm close to the house. You can jump out and check the house to see if Augie and Phyllis are inside. Make it quick and get back here so we can decide what to do." Just about that time Debbie hit a large bump and her little car went flying!

In a panic Joann screamed, "What was that?" Just about that time they crashed through the front of the house and slid to a stop. Joann was shook and started laughing as hard as she could. "I don't think you could get any closer, do you?" Debbie sat there stunned. "Wake up Debbie! We need to get out of here now!" Joann shook Debbie's shoulder.

As the dust settled Joann and Debbie saw a terrified Augie and Phyllis tied to chairs right in front of them. "Oh!" Yelled Debbie, "I could have run them over!" Joann and Debbie both jumped out of the car and cut them loose. Before they knew it bullets started flying. All four hit the floor. Debbie crawled to the driver side of the car and managed to get inside. Joann, Phyllis and Augie crawled to the car as well. They were almost in when Debbie started the car. Augie still had the door open and one foot on the floor of the house when Debbie floored the gas pedal and backed out of the house.

In a panic he drew himself into the car and managed to shut the door as they flew off the front porch. "Thank goodness we didn't put a tree there or you would be goners." Augie squealed. Phyllis was rendered speechless as she sat in the back hanging onto him.

Augie informed Debbie there was another way to the highway. He didn't think anyone but he and Phyllis knew about. "The road will take you to the other side of town and connect to the highway about 10 miles out." They flew out of the yard with several men firing guns at them.

Debbie was trying to go faster. "What is their problem? They can't even hit us."

Joann started laughing, "Some kind of bad guys can't hit anything."

Phyllis was ducking down in the back seat and replied in a panic, "I certainly hope they can't hit us."

Augie was trying to console Phyllis, "I don't think they are trying that hard to hit us, just scare us."

Phyllis sat up, "They don't have to scare us, Debbie is doing a fine job of scaring us all by herself."

Augie looked behind them. "No one is following us. When those goons apprehended us, I overheard them talking about a map. They must think we have it."

"We do have the map, Augie." Debbie replied. "Where is the road they might not know about? I'm exhausted from running from these guys."

Augie looked around, "It's just around the next bend in the road. When you cross the bridge, go about twenty feet and then back up off the road into the dry riverbed. First, slow down just before the bridge so we can see if anyone is following." Debbie slowed down when she reached the bridge. Augie told her it was clear and to turn off her lights when she crossed the bridge.

As soon as Debbie crossed the bridge she turned off her lights. Just past the bridge, she left the road going into the ditch and down to the dry riverbed. "What now, Augie?" Debbie asked, wondering which way to go.

Augie told her to park under the bridge as he exited the car. "Where are you going?" asked Joann.

"I'm going to get rid of some tracks. I'll be right back, keep the lights off." Augie shut the door and disappeared. Debbie drove down under the bridge and turned the car off. He hadn't been gone but a few minutes when they heard cars zoom past on the bridge.

It was another five minutes before Augie returned. He Tapped on Debbie's window and she about jumped out of her skin. "Shh…" Debbie said as she rolled down the window. "What are you doing, Augie? Get in the car!"

Augie whispered, "We are very vulnerable out here. This car is still visible to the road and the bridge until we get down the riverbed a ways. Don't step on your break, or open a door, or turn on the lights until I get us out of here. Slowly follow me, but keep the window down so you can hear me."

Debbie strained to see him walking in front of the car. "I can't see you Augie." Debbie leaned out the window. It was a very dark night. It took them about twenty minutes to get out of sight of the road and the bridge.

Finally, Aggie stopped and stepped aside as Debbie rolled up beside him. "Stop Debbie, I think we can turn on the headlights now and get going faster."

"Good we have to hurry and ditch or disguise this car soon. I can't have them follow us to where Dave and David are." Debbie commented as she stopped the car.

Augie opened the door of the car and got in quickly. Off they flew down a dirt road away from the farm. It took about an hour until they came to the highway.

As they approached the highway, Phyllis, who had been silent through most of the ordeal, said she had an idea. "Why don't we go back to Mobil Park City and the safety of our neighbors? They wouldn't dare do anything to us there, would they?" She suddenly became unsure. It was silent in the car as they drove up to the highway.

Debbie was anxious to see Dave and David, "I really need to get to Harmon, Dave and David are there with the authorities."

"Why didn't you say so in the first place?" Joann said excitedly.

Debbie put her hand on Joann's shoulder. "I guess I wasn't sure I should tell you, incase we were apprehended by the guys chasing us."

Joann put her hands on her hips and huffed, "I am getting pretty good at this espionage stuff. You could trust I wouldn't tell them anything if I were caught."

"I know, Joann, and I should have told you everything. I guess I was just to busy thinking of what to do next." Debbie apologized. "What is the quickest route to Harmon?"

Augie laughed, "You are on the highway, just turn left and get going!"

Debbie thanked Augie and off they flew as fast as they could go to Harmon.

# CHAPTER 11

*The streets* were quiet in the small town of Harmon, especially at one o'clock in the morning. As Debbie slowly drove down the main street, Joann asked where Dave and David were.

"They are in the garage at Joey's Auto Body Shop here. Strange I know, but it was the best place to lay low. We should be there in a few minutes; it's just outside Harmon on the west side. Keep your eyes open for anything suspicious."

They all looked around as Debbie drove down the street turning west and heading out of town. Augie spotted a dark vehicle parked in an ally. "I don't want to alarm anyone but I just saw a dark vehicle parked in the ally we just past."

Joann turned around looking, "Is it following us?"

Augie was still watching, "no it isn't." They all sighed but kept on their toes.

Debbie was excited, "Look up ahead there's Joey's Auto Body Shop. They pulled into the lot and up to the garage door clear at the back of the building. All was quiet, "I'll get out and look around." Debbie said nervously.

Augie cleared his voice, "No, you better not, I'll look around. The first sign of something wrong, you get out of here as fast as you can."

Phyllis grabbed Augie's arm, "I'll go with you."

Augie smiled, "No, you stay with them. If something is wrong here I don't want you to get hurt."

Phyllis grabbed his arm again. "I could get hurt riding with Debbie, she's a maniac behind the wheel of this car."

Augie patted Phyllis's hand, "It'll be okay, and I'll be right back." He got out of the car, while Debbie, Joann, and Phyllis sat there and watched him.

Debbie tapped the steering wheel with her finger. "I only wanted to save you and Augie not hurt you Phyllis."

Phyllis reached up and patted Debbie's shoulder, "I'm sure you didn't want to hurt us." Phyllis chuckled for a second relaxed but nervous. "You should have seen your face. I think you were as shocked as we were. I'm still a little shook, I've never seen you like this before."

Joann put her hand on Debbie's arm and smiled to reassure her everything would go fine.

Debbie pleaded under her breath, "Please, please, let Dave and David be here. I'm tired of running."

Sure enough Dave and David were there. The garage door opened and Debbie drove the car into the garage. They were all so very happy to finally be somewhat safe. Debbie, Joann, and Phyllis climbed out of the car and what a joyous reunion it was. Everyone wanted to tell his or her version of the story. Dave just looked at Debbie's car, "What on earth happened to your car?"

They all looked at the car as Dave and David walked around examining it. No one was sure they should tell Dave what happened so they looked at Debbie. Debbie looked back at them, then sheepishly at Dave and David. "I, uh, was trying to create a diversion so we could rescue Phyllis and Augie, but it back fired on me and we crashed through the front wall of their house instead. I guess I stirred up so much dust, I couldn't even see where I was going. Then I exited the same way I came in." Debbie explained with reservation.

"She's a scary driver, Dave." Phyllis said shaking her head. "I'm glad we are finally here." As the group settled down everyone decided to get some sleep and talk more in the morning.

## CHAPTER 12

*Morning brought* more news. To everyone's astonishment, Dave and David were on top of the whole situation. Not only did David know of Archie's involvement with the bad agents, but much more. "Mom, we think we have more information concerning Al and Karen's disappearance. The head office contacted Al's mom after the lengthy search for clues turned up nothing. Apparently, Al and Karen called her and told her they were coming to see her again. When they didn't show up she tried to contact them. It's good Al let people know where he was. She said she had a suspicious conversation with Al just two days before his disappearance. She said he acted like he was talking to a business-person, not his mom. He also made the conversation short and impersonal. After further discussion with Al's mom, they found he was going to look at a mustang and never told her where he was. Now that is definitely not the normal Al."

David walked over to a map on the wall. "Their motor home was found abandoned in Sequence. I had some of my trusted agents ask around to see if anyone had noticed Al and Karen. They had photos to show people and one woman remembered Karen. She said Karen was really friendly. And there was a red mustang parked by the motor home. The woman noticed the mustang because it was a late model, real flashy and pretty. Apparently, Karen told the lady Al was interested in buying the car. Karen and Al were last seen in Sequence driving away in a red mustang with a large bald man. The woman wasn't sure how old he was but said he was much younger than Al and Karen. She also didn't know what nationality he was; he was dark but could have had a good tan. The information we received from the witness was inconclusive. Not even a license plate number. The best thing about this is we do know they were here and alive." David sat down disgusted.

Dave patted David's shoulder; "It's okay David I'm sure we'll find them soon."

Augie examined the map. "Do you have an educated guess where they might have taken Al and Karen?"

David smiled, "No, not even a good guess."

Debbie sat down by David, "maybe we can help you think of ideas."

Joann perked up, "We have the key and the map that these guys want. Why can't we go back to Mobil Park City and wait for them?"

David smiled, "We could, however Archie is in with my bad agents Smyth and Wessin. If they see us back in Mobil Park City it won't be long before this group of bad characters surrounds us. We believe they have already committed murder so to kill someone else probably won't be a problem. I don't want it to be anyone in Mobil Park City." Dave and Augie were in the corner having their own conversation about the situation. "Dad, do you and Augie have some brilliant ideas?" David questioned.

Augie and Dave walked over to David. Augie suggested, "I think Al and Karen were set up with the mustang. Everyone, especially Archie knows Al can't resist a mustang.

David thought for a moment. "It must have been a sweet ride for Al to get side tracked from the map. I agree they were set up; apparently they were followed when they left dad and mom at Canyon Lake Lodge and headed back to Al's mom's house. Dad and mom were followed too, however they drove directly to Mobil Park City and that put them where they could be watched. Dad and I had already drawn that conclusion." David remarked. "To your knowledge, mom, is everyone in Mobil Park City who should be?"

"I guess, why ask me? Aren't your agents there watching everyone?" Debbie asked bewildered.

David looked at Debbie rather funny. "Who was chasing you?"

Debbie looked at Joann, "I didn't know the men who were chasing us."

"Why are you asking us anyway?" Joann interrupted, " we tried not to get to close. Remember they were chasing us, and we were running!" Joann added.

Dave put his arm around Debbie, "it's okay girls, and Archie wasn't one of them. Archie isn't the mastermind either. David and I think Archie was drawn in by promises and false reports. I don't think he really knows who he's mixed up with and I'm sure Archie wouldn't go for killing."

Phyllis listened intently to all that was said. "Why don't you use Archie to catch the truly bad guys? If he's not so bad than maybe he would be willing to cooperate with the authorities."

David thought for a moment, "That's not a bad idea. There's a helicopter port in the back of the sheriffs office in Mobil Park City. We can fly in and visit Archie before the mystery men find out. I'll call Archie and ask if my agents Smyth and Wessin are there at the office. If not I'll have Archie go locate them. I'll tell Archie I'm flying in to talk to Smyth and Wessin about some recent discoveries on Al and Karen's disappearance. If that doesn't get his attention, I don't know what will."

"That's a good idea, David." Dave was anxious to get going. "Maybe we should call Pastor Gerry and Norma, or Vic and have them gather as many Mobil Park City residence together as possible and have them all meet us over at the sheriff's office. If we create a cover I don't think we will be in too much danger. The only thing the men want that have been chasing us is the map."

Joann perked up, "I'll call Vic and have him get started gathering the people."

Augie volunteered to call Pastor Gerry. David arranged for a helicopter to fly all of them to Mobil Park City, and then he called Sheriff Archie to arrange the meeting with agents Smyth and Wessin. It seemed so easy and everything fell right into place. Archie agreed to go get the two agents, while Pastor Gerry and Vic agreed to gather the citizens together. What could go wrong with the plan?

David thought about everything, plenty could go wrong and more could go right. Yet something was bothering him greatly. It wasn't the map he knew where it was. His mother had it, and she was with him. No, it was the people. David started examining the evidence on this case again. There was certainly something missing, but what was it? "Let me see the map, mom." David asked.

Debbie looked at David. "Is something wrong?"

"Yes, but I don't know what it is that's bothering me right now." David motioned to Debbie for the map. Debbie walked over to David and handed him the map. David laid it out on the table as everyone gathered around to see what he was looking for.

Dave asked Debbie if she found the symbol he had asked her to examine in the cave. She didn't answer as Dave walked over to the table to look at the map. After carefully examining the map, he looked back at Debbie for an answer to his question. "Yes, I did find the symbol you asked me to find in the cave. I also examined the area and the symbol."

Before Debbie could say more Dave stated; "It was a clue on the map, and through examination and research David and I decided maybe there was something at Trepid Falls." Dave smiled, "She saw the symbol I asked about. I remembered seeing these symbols," he pointed to some symbols on the map, "Remember last summer when we were swimming at the falls?" Debbie nodded her head yes. Dave continued… "We discovered an underground channel that led to a cave. Remember?"

Debbie looked at the symbols on the map. "I do remember the cave and the symbols we discussed at the time." Debbie pointed to the symbols that she remembered seeing. "You told me to look for the symbols when I was in the cave. I studied this one when I was there. It was huge and covered a five by five area." Debbie looked at everyone, "I found another map when I was in the cave." Debbie produced the second map, and laid it down on the table beside the first map.

Dave and David were astonished, as were the others. "Where did you find this map?" asked David.

Debbie sighed, "I found it in the cave. I don't think they are connected."

Dave was concerned about the two different maps. "What's on your mind David?"

David examined the maps carefully. "Look at these marks dad, what do you make of them?" Dave took the magnifying glass and looked closely. "If I didn't know better I would say these marks by the mountain looking sign were engineering signatures." Dave looked up at David concerned, "Is that what you were thinking?"

David moved a book over to Dave and pointed to a symbol. "I was thinking exactly what you are. This map isn't as old as the first map that Al and Karen found in his mother's cellar. It's made on leather that is similar, but not as old and the symbols are like the ones in this book. Only engineers use these that I know of. Unless the symbols are universal to other professions."

Dave stood up, "I think Al could tell us if we are right or not. Are the maps connected in any way that you can see?

David examined the maps further and so did everyone else. Phyllis noted that the star in the upper left hand corner was the same and that the shape of the maps was in fact pretty close to the same. "Do you suppose the same people made both maps?" questioned Phyllis.

David scratched his head, "It's not entirely impossible, however I don't know the age of either one of the maps, and without studying them further I can't say for sure." David rolled the maps up together and handed them to Debbie for safekeeping. "Right now we need to get to Mobil Park City. I'm sure the helicopter will be here any minute now." David cleaned up the area and prepared to leave.

## CHAPTER 13

By the time they arrived at the Helicopter-Port in Mobil Park City, Vic had all the towns people gathered at the sheriff's office. However, upon arrival David and those who were with him discover that Sheriff Archie hadn't gone to retrieve agents Wessin and Smyth. David was concerned, "Sheriff Archie why didn't you get my agents Smyth and Wessin over here like I asked you to do? He questioned.

The crowd was getting loud and confusion was brewing over why they were all there, coupled with the fact that Joann and Debbie had returned with Dave, David, Augie and Phyllis. Shouts came from the crowd, "Why are we here? What's going on? What happened to Karen and Al?"

Vic climbed on a chair and shouted... "Quiet!" The crowd settled down.

Maxine concerned and frustrated over what she had been hearing about her husband, Sheriff Archie, pushed through the crowd to him. "What's going on Archie?" She questioned. "Is it true what I've been hearing about you?" Maxine was disturbed over the whole ordeal. Sheriff Archie looked down, ashamed to look at Maxine in the eye. "Well?" She insisted.

Sheriff Archie looked up and scanned the faces of his friends and neighbors. "I'm so ashamed!" He cried out, without thinking that anyone else could be mixed up in this mess. "They told me no one would get hurt if I cooperated, that I would be rewarded for helping. I had no idea they would hurt anyone. I'm worried for Al and Karen too. I think they are okay, but I'm not sure." Archie hung his head in shame. The crowd got upset and began to rumble again.

David held up his hand to quiet everyone. Vic yelled..."Quiet!"

Maxine smacked Archie's arm with the back of her hand. "Archie, how could you betray our friends and neighbors like this? How could you betray me like this!" Maxine huffed and shook her head.

Archie took Maxine's hand, "I'm so sorry dear, I was trying to make extra money without thinking about what I was really doing, or who it would effect."

David approached Sheriff Archie, "What you have done is get mixed up in kidnapping, murder, attempted murder, and the list goes on. As an agent, I have to arrest you. However, if you help us find Al and Karen and the leader of the people chasing us, there's a chance they'll go easy on you, maybe.

Sheriff Archie turned to the crowd, "I'm so sorry for what I have done. I know you won't trust me to guard and protect you anymore. I understand I have broken your trust and I apologize from the deepest part of my heart. Maxine and I love every one of you here at Mobil Park City, and you are more to us than friends, you are our family. I hope you can find it in your hearts to forgive me."

David looked around the room and noticed Gene wasn't there anymore. "I think something could foil our plan if we don't act quickly. Where did Gene go?"

Marlene looked around, "He must have gone to get Wessin and Smyth your agents."

David turned to Sheriff Archie, "You, dad and Willie go over to the Red Sparrow Inn and assist Gene. I'm not sure his motives are to help!"

Marlene got upset, "What do you mean, Gene wouldn't turn on everyone like Archie!"

Maxine burled up, "Archie didn't mean any harm! And how would you know Gene isn't mixed up in this, he talks to those two agents all the time." Maxine was hurt that Marlene was so insensitive.

David held his hand up as the crowd began to grumble at what they were hearing. "Settle down, no one knows for sure what Gene is doing. And Archie didn't turn on us he just had a moment of greed and bad decisions." Archie hung his head in shame. "We'll soon see what Gene's motives are." David stated as he and everyone walked out to the front of the Sheriff's office.

Suddenly a car flew around the corner, it must have been doing 90 mph, as it flew past the Sheriff's office. It wasn't a minute later when two pickup trucks and a black Lincoln flew around the same corner pushing speeds of the first car. Everyone watched as each and every vehicle flew past. Debbie, Joann, Augie, and Phyllis realized the trucks and the black Lincoln could have been the same vehicles that had chased them.

Joann made her way over to David. "I think those were the guys at Tripod Falls meeting with Sheriff Archie. The vehicles look like the same ones." Joann was excited.

David looked at Joann, "The first car was a red Mustang. Do you think Al and Karen are in it?" David looked over at his mom who was trying to see where the first car went. "What is it mom?" David asked.

Debbie looked back at David just as the red car flew around the corner again, and skid to a stop right in front of the Sheriff's office. Everyone stood there in surprise as Al and Karen jumped out of the car yelling, "Help, help us!" Al and Karen gasped for air, as they realized everyone in Mobil Park City was there in front of the Sheriff's office. "What is everyone doing here at the Sheriff's office?" Al gasped again.

Karen started crying, "You'll never believe what happened to us!" She struggled to gain her composure.

Al grabbed David, "Some really bad guys are after us. You have to do something!" Before David could answer Al, the two trucks and Lincoln came flying around the corner and came to an abrupt stop. As the men in the vehicles in question jumped out, all the people of Mobil Park City took a stand.

David was surprised to see they were agents and the Director of the FBI.

"What are you men doing?" David asked as he stepped in front of the crowd.

Al and Karen both yelled… "They were chasing us!"

Director Daniels stepped forward, "David, this car was reported stolen. When it crossed the roadblock that you asked for entering Mobil Park City we naturally tried to stop it. This man ran our roadblock and exceeded the speed limit going 98 mph. His suspicious behavior led us to believe we were in pursuit of your suspect. Where's the Sheriff?" Director Daniels asked.

David looked back at Al and Karen, then back at Director Daniels. "Sir, I didn't order a road block." David was getting uneasy, "This is Al and Karen the two kidnapped victims we have been looking for the last two weeks. Now we have them safe and sound maybe they can shed some light on what's really going on. You might want to stay and arrest two rouge agents, Smyth and Wessin. They are apparently mixed up in these crazy events. And possibly a few Mobil Park City citizens."

Marlene rushed forward grabbing David's arm. "Not Gene! He hasn't done anything!"

David patted Marlene's hand. "I'm sure we'll get all this sorted out, don't panic Marlene."

Debbie gave a concerned glance Joann's way. Joann nodded in concern. Debbie moved through the crowd slowly toward David trying not to draw attention. Joann tried to move that direction too. Debbie realized it would be hard not to be noticed, so she watched Joann until Joann finally looked her way. Debbie mouthed, "stop!" to her and pointed to the ground. They both shook their heads okay and ducked down to the ground. Joann was giggling, trying not to be loud when her and Debbie met in the midst of the crowd.

Phyllis was standing there; she looked around to see if anyone noticed her, then ducked down to see what was going on. "Why are you crawling around on the ground?" Phyllis asked.

Debbie looked up at Augie and motioned to Phyllis to pull him down where they were. Phyllis grabbed Augie's leg. He jumped "Ah…" then he looked around smiled and tried to hide himself from the agents. Then he too ducked down to see what was going on. "Phyllis, why did you grab my leg? It surprised me and I think I attracted attention." Augie was concerned too.

Debbie whispered, "Don't you recognize these guys at all?"

Phyllis and Augie stood up slowly and studied the agents and the Director as he talked to David. Then they slipped down to the ground again. Augie and Phyllis agreed they hadn't seen them before at all. Augie told Debbie… "We don't recognize them at all. They aren't the ones that were at our house wrecking it."

Phyllis in her quiet matter of fact voice said, "actually our house didn't get wrecked until Debbie arrived and drove her car through the house to rescue us."

Debbie looked at Phyllis, "I'm sorry, I didn't plan on crashing into the house it was an accident. I really…"

Joann interrupted, "Excuse me but at the moment we need to tackle more important business. These are the guys we saw at Trepid Falls and David needs to know. Agents, Director, or not they met with Archie and are in fact bad guys."

Augie was beside himself, "Is the whole agency corrupt? No offense, but your son David is in for trouble if everyone is on the take. He's going to need all the help he can get." Augie shook his head in disgust.

About that time Glenn squatted down and joined the group. "What is cooking down here? Don't you find what's happening up there more interesting?"

"No!" Debbie, Joann, Phyllis, and Augie whispered all together in frustration.

Glenn drew away slightly. "Sorry, what is the problem?"

Joann looked at Glenn, "These guys are the ones we saw at Trepid Falls when Debbie and I went to meet Dave and David. They chased us, and the story is long, so some other time we will tell you more." Joann, Debbie, Phyllis, and Augie went back to talking.

Glenn joined the huddle again. "I have an idea, why don't we tell everyone here so no one else gets hurt. Don't you think it would be a good idea if everyone knew."

They all thought about the suggestion. Debbie turned to Glenn; "It would be a good idea to inform everyone so we'll let you do that. I'm going to call David on his cell phone. I can't get to him to say anything without them seeing me so that's the only way I think." Debbie dialed the phone and told David about the agents and the Director. David thanked her and hung up. Glenn, Augie, and Phyllis stood up and watched the agents and David during the conversation.

Phyllis happened to see Al and Karen they looked worried. Phyllis joined Debbie and Joann on the ground once again. "I think Al and Karen are afraid. They look worried and frantic for somewhere to go."

Debbie and Joann were worried. Debbie asked Phyllis and Augie to make their way over to them and let them know she had told David they were the same agents that had been chasing them. Debbie grabbed Phyllis's arm, "Only if you're sure those agents don't know you."

Phyllis smiled, "We're sure, don't worry." Augie and Phyllis made their way over to Al and Karen.

Debbie stood up but bent over so she wouldn't be seen. She could see Phyllis and Augie get to Al and Karen. Debbie needed to see them know in their minds it would be okay. When she was sure she got back down on the ground. Then made a call to Dave so he would know as well. Joann and Debbie tried to make it to the back of the crowd. Once there they stood up and looked for a way to disappear safely.

It wasn't long when Dave, Willie, Sheriff Archie, and Gene showed up with agents Smyth and Wessin. Director Daniels and his agents arrested Wessin and Smyth. "We'll put these two under high security and hold them for you to debrief." Director Daniels informed David.

"Thanks Sir." David shook his hand. Then turned to the crowd, "It's important for you to know that the investigation into the series of events the last month is not over. I want everyone here to know how important it is to stay alert and watch out for each other. I don't want anyone else missing." The crowd started to dissipate and David shook Sheriff Archie's hand whispering, "It's not over Archie, so watch your back. Help me and I will make sure you're taken care of." David winked at Sheriff Archie and walked over to his dad.

Marlene was clinging onto Gene and hoping they might have given up their suspicions of him. Dave walked up to Gene and put his hand on Gene's shoulder, "Thanks Gene, for getting over to the Inn and retaining Wessin and Smyth until we arrived." Gene looked at Dave and nodded. Dave and David exchanged a look and David told everyone to return to their homes. As they all left to go home everyone hugged Al and Karen and told them they were glad they were back safe.

Dave and David told Karen and Al they didn't want them out of their sight. "Surely the agents and your Director will do something soon. They know, we know, who kidnapped us." Al spoke in a low voice.

David was concerned that all would come to a head and he didn't know if there were any agents left to trust. "Don't worry to much, we'll just stick together. They know mom and Joann as well; they saw the agents down at Trepid Falls meeting with Sheriff Archie.

Al was shocked, "Sheriff Archie met with the agents? I can't believe it. Did he know of them kidnapping us?" Al asked.

David smiled at Al, "Yes, he knew. Archie said he was told no one would get hurt. Archie feels bad and will help us now. He has to be careful or he could get hurt, these guys mean business."

Karen leaned over and whispered, "What do they want with all of us? Does it have anything to do with the map?"

David sighed, "I am not sure right now but the map may or may not have a bearing on these incidents. Don't worry, we'll get to the bottom of this soon." David tried to be reassuring.

Vic strolled over to Dave, David, Al and Karen. "Have you seen Joann?"

Dave looked around, "No, Debbie is missing too."

David smiled and taped Dave on the shoulder, "Don't look or point but mom and Joann are over there in the bushes." Then David looked around to see if the agents and Director had left. "Don't draw attention to them just yet, Director Daniels is over there talking to one of his agents." David walked over to the Director, "Did you take the agents, Smyth and Wessin into the agency?" David asked.

Director Daniels looked at David, "Yes we did, do you want help here?"

David decided they were waiting to nab Al and Karen again. "No I still have a few agents I can trust. Thanks anyway. I'll be into the agency the end of the week to debrief agents Smyth and Wessin."

Director Daniels realized he had to be moving along to avoid suspicion "Yes, well we'll be seeing you then." He and the agent with him got into their car and left.

As soon as they were out of sight Debbie and Joann ran over to Dave and everyone. "Whoa, I was afraid those agents would see us. We need to go home or somewhere where they can't see us."

David suggested they all stick together since the agents and Director may be looking to get rid of anyone who can point them out in court. All of a sudden Debbie, Joann, Al and Karen were quiet. "I don't know but you do, you are all eye witnesses to some of their activities. They won't want you to live to testify." David felt for them all and knew he had to protect them.

Dave was now concerned, "I think Augie and Phyllis are in danger as well. They would still be with the guys that had them tied up at their farm if Debbie and Joann hadn't freed them. Where did they go?

Debbie looked around. "I saw them in the crowd, maybe they left with Harley and Carol."

Dave looked at David, "where do we hide them, David?

David thought for a minute. "I have an Island no one knows about. I'll hide them there."

They were all shocked, "You what?"

David put his hands in the air, "Get in the car, we'll talk somewhere safer than here. Dad go get Augie and Phyllis and I'll meet you back at my place." Dave took off to check the Red Sparrow Inn and everyone got into the car. David continued, "I have an Island no one knows about."

Debbie interrupted David, "How can you have an Island no one knows about?"

David sighed, "I do, you didn't know about it did you? I have worked for the agency long enough to know that sometimes you need a place no one knows about and it's safe." Everyone sat in the car in surprise and rather speechless. David proceeded to tell them they needed to get the bare essentials from their homes and he would have some of his agents watch their houses. "When dad and I figure out what to do then we will contact you. Don't under any circumstances take a cell phone or any other devise that can be traced to you. Computers are out, sorry."

Debbie frowned, "How long do we have to hide, David?"

David reassured her it wouldn't be long. "Vic, I want you to go too.

They might try to use you to get to Joann so you need to stay together." David advised. "When you get your stuff be sure to leave a light on in your house. It needs to look like you are home at least for awhile." David looked at all of them and tried to look hopeful.

David took each of them to their houses and they collected what they could use and then he returned them to his house to wait until time to go. It wasn't long when Dave arrived at David's with Augie and Phyllis.

# CHAPTER 14

*The night* was dark and must have been overcast; there were no stars or moon to light the way. David and Dave took Joann, Vic, Al, Karen, Augie, Phyllis, and Debbie quietly out of town and on a strange journey to an island that David apparently owned, or at least knew about that no one else knew about. There they would be safe from the bad agents and who ever else was involved in the series of crimes. Dave and David were successful in getting them to the island safely and themselves back to town to David's house without incident.

Once back at home they decided to rest and then formulate a plan. They no sooner got to sleep, when they were woke by a crowd of people in their front yard pounding on the door. David stumbled out of bed, shaking from being wakened so abruptly from a short lived deep sleep and answered the door. "What do you want?" David rubbed his eyes.

Donna & Bob stepped forward as Donna nudged Bob's arm. "We haven't seen Karen, Al, Debbie, or your dad since last night. What has happened to them?" Bob asked as the crowd agreed with the question.

Glenn spoke up. "I went over to Al and Karen's house this morning and no one answered the door. We are all concerned about their safety."

David squinted his eyes for lack of sleep. Rubbing his head, he looked the crowd over. Buried in the crowd were two agents of questionable character. David looked back in his house as Dave appeared in the doorway.

Dave was rubbing his eyes too. "They were afraid, this wasn't the end of strange people chasing them and perhaps kidnapping them again."

David held his hand up, "Please, dad, I'll handle this. "Mom," David shook his head, "Mom, Debbie as you know her, took Al and Karen to a place they can all feel safe."

Bob looked around, "What about Joann and Vic, where are they?"

Carol yelled from the back of the crowd. "Augie and Phyllis are gone too."

David and Dave realized this could get a bit complicated, David noticed the rouge agents headed to a car. "Joann and Vic chose to go with them and help Debbie protect them." David was anxious to follow the agents that had left the crowd.

Glenn was concerned, "We can all help protect them. They didn't have to leave. We need to stick together and see this resolved." Glenn was agitated as well.

Harley spoke up, "Maybe you could just have Debbie bring them back and we could all stay at the Red Sparrow until it's safe for everyone to return home."

David turned to his dad, "Dad you handle this, I have to go, something is up and I need to look into it." David went back into his house.

Dave looked slightly pressed, "Look everyone, it's not a bad idea for all of you to stay at the Red Sparrow until we solve this case. I need to help David and I'm sure Debbie, Al, Karen, Vic, Joann, Augie and Phyllis will be safe. I'll let you know more as I find out more. Until then I'll see you." Dave returned to the house and disappeared inside shutting the door.

Glenn was upset about Dave's abruptness, "Well, that's just stupid! What do we do now?"

Bob in his ever so calm voice suggested they all get what they need and meet at the Red Sparrow Inn. "I think it's a good idea for us to stay close and wait. If something is going to happen, Dave and David or even Debbie and the others will contact us there."

Glenn scowled, "Well that's just stupid! How will they know we are all there, or that we are okay?" Donna grabbed Glenn's arm, "Come on Glenn, they'll know we are at the Red Sparrow because Dave told us to go there."

Cindy laughed, "Are you worried we will hear you dreaming again, Glenn?" Everyone laughed and joked as they headed out to get their things and meet at the Red Sparrow Inn.

Glenn huffed, "No I don't plan on dreaming or sleeping until this mess is settled." Once again everyone had a good laugh.

# CHAPTER 15

*The morning* sun peeked up over the mountain all to soon. Debbie sat in the window watching the sunrise. Joann, Karen and Phyllis happened to be coming down the stairs and noticed Debbie gazing out the window. "Are you okay, Debbie?" Joann asked.

Debbie sighed turning and looking at the inquisitive faces looking back at her. "Yes," she smiled. "Did you have a good sleep?" Questioned Debbie.

Joann, Karen and Phyllis studied Debbie for a moment. Karen looked at Joann then back at Debbie "I slept great and I haven't slept that well for a long time." Karen smiled so unsuspecting. She felt the mood of the other three was quite different. "What's going on with you?" Karen asked.

Joann whipped around and started walking off. "Oh no! No way, Debbie!" Joann boomed out of the room toward the kitchen of the little cabin.

Karen was confused, "What's going on with you two? Debbie," she looked strangely into Debbie's face. "You are grinning and Joann is yelling, what is going on!" insisted Karen as she hurried after Joann.

"You know we can't just sit here and do nothing, Joann. Admit it, you don't like being here any more than I do." Debbie said following Joann and Karen into the kitchen. Vic and Al were sitting at the kitchen table eating cereal and hesitated when the women entered the kitchen. "Joann, you haven't even heard my idea yet." Debbie pleaded.

Joann slapped her hand on the counter as Phyllis walked into the kitchen. "Ha! What idea? You didn't share any idea, or plan the last time I went running across country with you. And you practically totaled your car with me in it! What idea, Debbie? You don't share plans or ideas!" Joann poured herself some juice and sat down at the table with Al and Vic who up to that moment had their mouths open in shock.

Augie looked wide-eyed at the women as Phyllis went over to him in an almost desperate manner. Nervously he asked, "So you are planning on another adventure? I'm glad you don't have a car."

Vic and Al were a bit confused not knowing of the adventures Joann and Debbie had embarked upon in the last few days. "What is going on?" Questioned Vic calmly.

Karen sat down by Al looking at both Joann and Debbie with interest. "I'd like to know too." She added.

Al put down his spoon. "Maybe we all need to know what is up with you two."

Debbie went over to the table and joined everyone. "For the past few days, Joann and I have been moving around trying to protect the maps and find Dave and David. We also saved Augie and Phyllis from their captures."

Joann interrupted, "No, for the past few days we have been running around being shot at, crawling through dirty bushes, crashing cars into houses, and on the run from people we don't even know. We don't know who is bad and who is good. And all the time Debbie is in full control of the plans and not sharing where we are going or what we are doing. I'm tired and don't want to run anymore."

Vic put his arm around Joann to console her. "Now, Joann, I don't think it could have been that bad."

Phyllis interrupted Vic, "Oh yes it was! Debbie crashed her car through our house stopping inches from Augie and I. Of course I think it was an accident. I don't think she planned to drive in and get us. She looked as shocked as we were."

Debbie put her hand on Joann's arm. "I'm sorry I didn't exactly tell you everything I was thinking. However, crashing into Augie and Phyllis's house was not apart of my plan at all. It was an accident." Debbie looked at Augie and Phyllis, "I am sorry for that. It did turn out better than one might have expected in the long run though, don't you think?" Debbie tried to convince everyone.

Al and Karen were in disbelief. "What are you saying?" Al broke into the conversation. "You drove a car into a house?" Al was shocked, "are you crazy?"

Karen chimed in, "Into Augie and Phyllis's house!" Karen just shook her head. "To think we were having it bad."

Debbie looked at Al and Karen, "For your information, the guys that had kidnapped you, had Augie and Phyllis tied up and the entire farm was surrounded by gunmen. What were we supposed to do? Leave them to disappear too?" Debbie was frustrated by this time.

Augie in his quiet manner smiled. "It was good to be saved. Shocking, but good."

Phyllis sat down by Augie, "If these people come for us again, I am glad we are with someone who will fight to escape and not get caught. Not to mention won't leave one of us behind. If I have to sacrifice my home to escape it's a small loss."

Joann put her arm around Debbie, "No, we were supposed to do exactly what we did. I'm sorry I just went off the deep end. When I saw that silly grin on your face it reminded me of when you thought you had a great plan to rescue them and it went crazy." Joann just sighed.

Vic was silently taking in all the conversation. They all just sat around the table thinking in silence. Then Vic broke the silence, "What did Dave and David say to us when they left us last night?"

Al looked at Vic, "Is that a trick question?"

Debbie stood up and walked over to the sink. "They said to sit tight until they call us or come to get us."

Vic smiled, "Yes! So we will do just that. No leaving. We will do exactly what they told us to do."

Debbie stared out the kitchen window. "I am worried, what if something happens to them?"

Al tried to be positive, "We will wait a few days. They will be back soon, I'm sure of it. Didn't they give you the map?"

Debbie turned and looked at Al. "Yes, why?"

Al smiled, "We can study the map and maybe we will know where to look when they come back for us."

Debbie stared at Al for a moment. "Didn't they tell you?"

"Tell me what?" Al questioned.

Debbie walked back to the table, "Tell you there are two maps!"

Al looked surprised, then confused. "I knew there was a possibility of another map. That's when Karen and I left you at Canyon Lake Lodge and returned to my mother's place. Or should I say, tried to return to mothers when we were kidnapped."

Debbie pulled both maps from her pocket. "Here is the map you gave us to hold onto and here is the other map. Dave and David guessed where it was and had me retrieve it. That's where I went when Joann insisted on going with me."

Joann held up both hands, "Hold it, hold it, I believe it was a good thing I went with you, or you would have joined Al and Karen in being kidnapped. And the maps would not be here now if I hadn't."

Debbie laughed, "This is true. That's when we also found out how dirty Archie was."

Al and Karen were in disbelief. "What? Archie. Bad? He couldn't have had a part in our kidnapping, could he?" Exclaimed Al.

Karen just shook her head, "Pour Maxine, she must be devastated."

"Don't worry they have all that under control now. Here are the two maps. Dave and David think that the second map is peculiar because of the odd symbols. They were going to ask you about them when the time was right. What do you think, Al?" Debbie put the maps out on the table and everyone looked at them. She pointed out the strange symbols. "David said they look like engineering symbols not ancient Indian symbols. What do you think?"

Al studied the symbols, "They look similar but not quite. It looks like the person that made this map took some engineering symbols and changed them to confuse the map reader if by chance the map should get into the wrong hands."

Debbie studied the maps. "Do the maps go together?"

Al scratched his head, "I don't know. It looks as though they could go together and then it doesn't." Al looked up at everyone. "I guess we'll just have to figure them both out to know."

Debbie studied the maps some more. "You know, I think I know where the map leads to. I've already been there!" She exclaimed.

Everyone looked startled. Joann thought for a moment, "Was I with you?"

Before Debbie could answer they all heard a motorboat in the distance. Al rushed to the window with Vic and the others close behind him. "What do you make of it Al?" questioned Vic.

Al grabbed some field glasses that had been on the bookcase and examined the situation. Debbie went back to the table, collected the maps and stashed them safely in her pocket. Then grabbed her jacket, and proceeded to hand the others their jackets. Al put the glasses back on the bookcase and turned facing everyone. "Don't worry its just Dave and David. I think we can relax." Al suggested.

As everyone started putting their jackets back on the hanging hooks by the door, Debbie excitedly said, "Don't put your jackets away. Get ready to leave. Dave and David just left us last night, it's now morning, something is wrong with this picture."

Al hesitated as the others had already hung theirs up. "What could be wrong here? It's Dave and David and they are seemingly alone."

"Don't you think it would take them much longer to clear up things? Twelve hours or so doesn't exactly seem long enough for me to feel comfortable with this. It wouldn't hurt to be a little careful, considering the past few weeks." Debbie suggested.

Vic walked over to the window where he could see the dock and landing that led up to the cabin. "I can see the boat and Dave and David are getting out of the boat. It doesn't look like anyone is with them or following them."

Karen and Joann agreed it would be a good idea to at least keep watch just in case. So Vic kept watching as Dave and David made their way to the cabin. As they approached the door Debbie opened it. "Why are you back so soon?" She asked. They walked into the cabin and Debbie shut the door.

Dave turned and hugged Debbie as he told her to quit worrying.

They all went and sat down. David told them he had contacted the head office to report all the rouge agents and the Director as well. "It is in our best interest to sit tight until we hear from the top agency in charge of all the agents." David announced. "I don't think it will take long. I told them everything, dad and I made sure our friends and family will be safe during this time. We told all of them to stay at the Red Sparrow Inn until they heard from us."

The men we are dealing with don't want to draw any more attention to themselves then they already have. Kidnapping and murder are not their goal. The map is what they want and so you seven are in more danger than the others." David continued. "Right now they are not sure which one of you has the map in their possession. I want to keep it that way for now."

Debbie could no longer be silent. "I know where to go to start looking for the treasure, Dave." She looked anxious, Dave and the others looked at her waiting for more information.

Finally they all said, "where?"

David stopped Debbie, "No don't say it. We can't go treasure hunting until this matter of bad agents is cleared up. I don't want anyone getting hurt by greedy curious fellows who would kidnap or kill to get their hands on the map. So I suggest you keep your thoughts, and ideas of where to look under your cap until this other matter is closed, please."

Debbie shrugged her shoulders but agreed to hold her tongue until a more calm and safe time should arrive. Al's curiosity got the better end of him. "Why can't we just discuss it among ourselves? What can that hurt?" Al asked David.

David shook his head. "What if there's a breech in our plan and the bad agents get their hands on one of us. Even if we don't happen to have the map we would have an idea and it's possible that they would get that information out of us."

Al hung his head, "He's right, they can be very persuasive. When we were in their clutches, they persuaded us to tell them where the map was. I think that's why they were after you, Debbie" Al apologized to her and Dave. "I didn't tell them we thought there was a second map though." Al felt that was a positive note.

Debbie smiled, "That's okay Al. They didn't catch up with me. I do think we need to keep a good eye on Joann and myself, as we were together the whole time, after our house was ransacked. She knows quite a bit too." Debbie looked over at Joann.

Joann nodded, "I do know to much. Like the fact that Debbie is really a maniac behind the wheel of a car and has far to many spy ideas in her head." Joann laughed, "I think soon we will see the humor in all this."

As the time passed they talked and laughed the afternoon away. As night overtook them it brought on another feeling of uncertainty. Dave and David decided to keep watch and not use lights at all. So they all settled in for a long night.

# CHAPTER 16

*Just before* dawn David received a phone call from the agency. He woke his dad who was sleeping quite sound. "Dad," David whispered. "Wake up, I need to talk to you."

Dave woke up and slipped out to the porch with David where they could talk without disturbing everyone. "What is it?" His dad asked.

"The agency called and all the agents on the list including the Director, were picked up last night. I'm not sure it's clear yet I need to go back to Mobil Park City and check it out. Do you think you could stay here for now?" David asked his dad.

"No," Dave replied. "Mom will be okay here. I think you need your back covered just incase things aren't as they should be. It'll just take me a minute and we can go. I need to tell your mom." Dave went back into the cabin and woke Debbie up. "Debbie," Dave whispered.

Debbie woke up startled thinking something was wrong. "What!"

"Shhh! " Dave calmed her down, "David and I need to return to Mobil Park City. David received a call from the agency stating that all agents and the Director were arrested last night. He wants to go see if you and the others will be safe if you return to Mobil Park City. I need to go with him. I don't feel comfortable with David returning alone.

You'll be okay here with Vic and everybody. We won't be long." Dave whispered as he kissed Debbie good-bye.

Debbie got up and put her shoes on. "Can I go with you?"

"No," Dave hugged Debbie, "You need to stay here where I know you are safe."

Debbie frowned, "You mean where you think I might be safe."

Dave looked into Debbie's eyes, "If someone arrives on this island you don't know, remember what David told you and get everyone out. Don't forget to call me if this happens. I have to go now, keep watch." Dave and David left and Debbie watched, as they made there way down to the dock onto the boat and gone. She wrapped up in a blanket to keep watch until daylight came and the others woke up.

After awhile Debbie started nodding off to sleep. She would jump and wake up, but then nod off to sleep again. About sunrise, Debbie was awakened by the sound of a motorboat. She jumped up and looked out the window. A boat was fast approaching the dock. Debbie grabbed the field glasses and tried to see who it was. All the others must have been awakened by the sound as well. They came running in to see what was going on.

Al immediately thought it was David and Dave leaving. "Where are Dave and David going?"

Debbie was studying the situation and said, "David and Dave left about four hours ago. They went to see if it would be safe to return to Mobil Park City. This is not Dave or David. I think we are in trouble guys!" Debbie tossed the field glasses onto the bookcase, ran over and locked the door. Grabbing her coat she yelled, "What are you waiting for we have to go! Now guys!" Debbie grabbed her backpack and headed out the back with Vic, Joann, Karen, Al, Augie and Phyllis close behind her.

They ran down a path for a few hundred yards and then ducked into some shrubs. They were moving fast and Debbie was trying to remember what David had told her if something like this should happen. Debbie stopped for a breath of air.

Vic walked back a few paces to check and see if they were still okay.

Joann was gasping for air, "I don't think I am prepared to go running around in the bush. Where do we go from here?" She asked as she tried to catch her breath.

Debbie was out of breath too, "David told me to follow his signs and it would lead us to a cave with some jet skies. We are to get out of here on those if the need arises." She gasped for air.

Al being short of breath as well, "Is this one of those times we need to escape on jet skies?" he was in a slight panic as he had never rode one before, and neither had Karen.

Debbie smiled, "It could be, we'll see what happens. Don't worry, Al, if we need to I don't think you will have trouble. You drive cars don't you?"

Vic returned, "I think we need to be quiet and keep moving." He motioned to Debbie. She acknowledged with a nod. Down through the bushes they went until they reached a dense wooded area. Debbie stopped and looked around. Everyone was quiet. Debbie found one of David's signs, they moved through the wooded area quickly and quietly as possible. Debbie led them to a rocky cliff. It jetted straight up about one hundred and fifty feet and was covered with vines and dense green bushes. Debbie studied the area walking up and down the cliff until she found what she was looking for, another sign. The others were resting while she looked. Vic kept a look out.

"Come on," Debbie quietly said to the others. "I believe it is through here." Into a small opening covered with thick green bushes they all disappeared into a dark damp crevasse. After covering the opening Debbie squeezed past the others. She had taken a flashlight out of her backpack and turned it on so they could see where to go.

Al looked surprised, "I see you came prepared."

Debbie shined the light down the narrow pathway of rocks. "David made sure I had everything we might need in the pack. Come on we need to go." The narrow rocky path was quite a ways, winding down. Not to rough and easy to maneuver for most. About a quarter mile down the path it widened and became damp dirt so the walking got easier. The path wound around about another quarter of a mile and they entered a big room behind a waterfall. There were four jet skies waiting for them. "Ah, we made it." Debbie sighed. "We should be on the opposite side of the island from the cabin. Dave told me to call if anyone came to the island." Debbie walked over to the far dark corner of the cave and began shuffling her feet as if to be looking for something.

Vic got up and went over to where she was. "What are you looking for?" He asked.

Debbie shined the flashlight around. "I'm looking for a short rope with a knot on the end of it. David told me there were blankets and supplies for us to use in case we didn't have to leave. There's also a special radiophone to call them." Debbie kept looking as Vic and Augie started looking too.

Joann came over to help look. "How will we know if we need to leave the island?

"David will tell me when I call him, or we will know our hiding place down here has been breeched. Either way I suppose will do it." Debbie said as she hunted for the rope.

Karen was sitting down on a rock, "How will we hear someone coming? The waterfall makes so much noise." She shivered, "I'm so cold."

Al walked over to Karen, "Don't worry we'll post a watch." He sat down beside Karen and tried to keep her warm.

Debbie finally found the rope and opened the trap door to a cellar that held some blankets and supplies, as well as the special radiophone. "Don't worry Karen we have blankets now." Debbie announced.

Debbie climbed down in the cellar and handed some blankets up to Vic and Joann. Joann took some over to Al, Karen, Augie and Phyllis.

After Debbie climbed out of the cellar she looked around. "We need to post a lookout. Who wants to be the first watchman?" She looked at everyone, "Well, do I have a volunteer?"

Joann looked around, "I'll take the first watch. How long should the shifts be?" She asked.

Vic in his ever-familiar concerned manner said, "I'll take the watch you need to stay here. I don't want you getting hurt."

Joann was indignant, "Hurt? Victor, I could have gotten hurt in the car riding with Debbie. I think if I can survive that ride I can certainly take care of myself keeping watch!" She stood there with her hands on her hips as if to say, (Don't you dare tell me I can't help!)

Debbie was amused, and upset, "Why do you constantly bring up the ride in my car? I got things done didn't I?" Debbie shook out her blanket and wrapped it around her shoulders.

Joann giggled, "Yes you did and in a memorable way at that! I'm sorry I brought it up again. I'll try not to bring it up to many times." She giggled again as she walked to the tunnel they had entered the cave from. "Should I go part of the way down this tunnel?" Joann asked.

Vic threw his blanket over his shoulders and promptly walked to Joann. "I'm going with you, I think we need to keep watch in twos. Don't you think?" Joann wasn't opposed to that idea, as she didn't want to go into the damp tunnel alone.

Augie threw a blanket over his shoulders. "I'll go help Vic so Joann can stay here with Debbie. They might need to get out quickly and I know Debbie can do that."

Debbie sat down, "I think that is a good idea, just don't make a lot of noise. Oh, before you go we need to discuss our escape incase we need to do so fast. There are only four jet skies, so I think Karen should ride with Al and I can ride one so I guess Vic and Joann should be on one and Phyllis and Augie on the other. What do you think?" Debbie looked at the others for their reaction and ideas.

Al thought it was a good idea. Karen was relieved she didn't have to drive one but Joann voiced her concern. "I wanted to ride one alone."

Vic butted in, "Oh no, I will drive us." Joann wrinkled her nose.

Augie looked at the jet skies, "I've driven these before so I think Phyllis and I will be okay."

Debbie looked at everyone, "Okay, it's settled. Go keep watch and I'll call David." The phone rang and rang, Debbie decided to try David's cell phone.

A couple rings later David picked up the phone, "Hello," David answered in a whisper, "Hello!" He said again.

Debbie replied, "David, it's me, mom. Are you okay?"

There was silence for a couple seconds, "Yes, where are you, Mom?" David whispered.

"We had to leave the nest, someone came to us but it wasn't you." Debbie paused.

David started laughing, "I thought something had happened to you. It was dad and I; we're here at the nest trying to figure out if someone had flushed you out. Stay put we're going to have a look around. Don't expect us to find you in the obvious manner. Now hang up and store the radio, we'll see you soon." Debbie put the radiophone away and stored it back in the cellar.

Climbing out of the cellar Debbie was thinking about earlier that morning when the boat arrived. She could swear it wasn't David and Dave. Al noticed Debbie had a stern look on her face. "What's wrong, Debbie?"

Debbie looked up at Al and Karen sitting on a rock wrapped up in a couple blankets. "Did you get a good look at the boat that arrived before we took off out the back of the house?" Debbie asked.

Al slowly shook his head, "No, why?"

"I just talked to David and he and Dave are here on the island, at the house. I think I need to go ask Vic if he took a good look at the guys that got out of the boat." Debbie felt very uneasy.

Al got up quickly, "No, Debbie, I'll go ask him. You wait here." Al took off down the tunnel.

Debbie tried to stop him, "Wait, Al, why should I wait here?"

Al emerged from the tunnel. "Someone needs to get Karen out of here if we are all in danger. I think you could do that." He started to leave.

"Not any better than you, Al. I thought I saw strangers arriving at the boat dock; there were three of them not two. I think David and Dave are in trouble and so are we." Debbie looked at Al confused.

Al told Debbie to stay with Karen, Phyllis and Joann he said he would talk to Augie and Vic. "If there's danger, I'll yell real loud. You won't miss read it I promise. You have the maps and know how to read them, it's important that you, Karen, Phyllis and Joann get out of here safe. If something is up just try to get to the Red Sparrow Inn, everyone else is waiting there for things to settle down." Al disappeared into the tunnel.

Debbie paced up and down by the mouth of the tunnel. The other gals watched Debbie for a short while then got frustrated at her pacing. Karen got down from the perch she was on and walked over to Debbie.

She just stood there looking at her. "Stop pacing! You're making me nervous."

Debbie stopped pacing and looked at Karen. "I should have talked to David more. I should have asked him questions like, was there another boat when they arrived at the dock. Or what time did you get here. Something to make sure this island isn't getting crowded, or worse yet make sure it was really David!" Debbie started pacing again.

Joann walked over and grabbed Debbie by the shoulders, "You did fine. David and Dave can take care of themselves. They have proved that to all of us over and over. Let's just be ready for anything and we'll be okay."

Debbie stopped pacing again. "You're right, go over to the jet skies and be ready. I'm going to slip down the tunnel for a short ways and listen. If I come charging out jump on the jet skis and get ready to ride!" Debbie started to enter the tunnel.

Karen looked panicked, "Debbie, I can't drive one of those!"

Debbie looked back at her and stopped, "No, you can't. I have a better idea. Let's set a trap for whoever comes out of this tunnel."

Karen got excited for a moment and then… "Oh wait! What if Vic, Augie and Al come out of the tunnel first?" Karen had a way of thinking about these things.

Debbie smiled, "Then we will all escape on the jet skies. If not then we will have a good plan to capture whoever is giving us trouble and have a bargaining chip." Debbie started to arrange her plan.

Phyllis walked over to help Debbie, "What would we need a bargaining chip for?"

Debbie kept working on her plan. "Let's just take one step at a time. I plan better on the go anyway." Phyllis looked worried as Debbie climbed down into the cellar. "Should I go down there with you?" Phyllis asked.

Debbie looked up at Phyllis, "No, just keep watch, and when I hand stuff to you be ready to take it." Debbie proceeded down the ladder.

Debbie handed Phyllis some weapons, ammo, ropes and bungee cords. Joann and Karen decided to help Debbie too.

Karen looked at the items with amusement. "What are you going to do with bungee cords?" Karen began to giggle.

"Don't you worry about what I'm going to do with it just take it?" Debbie was agitated, and finally climbed out of the cellar and closed the door and hid all the signs of it's existence.

"What now?" Karen enquired, as she looked around.

Debbie looked around as well, "Let's take this stuff over behind the rocks." Debbie gathered a hand full and Joann, Phyllis and Karen gathered the rest. "Karen, hand me one of your blankets."

Karen looked upset, "No, it's cold down here."

Debbie stood up and took hold of one of the blankets Karen was wrapped up in. "Don't worry, pretty soon you'll be all heated up with excitement and won't want either blanket, come on give it up!"

Karen reluctantly gave the blanket to Debbie. "If Al, Vic and Augie come out first and it's a leave quick situation, what do you think we should do with these guns and ammo?" She looked inquisitively at Debbie.

Debbie jerked Karen down behind the rocks. "Leave it to you to question everything." She shoved a loaded gun into Karen's hands as Joann and Phyllis loaded some of the other guns.

Karen looked at the gun and then at Debbie in a panic. "The bad guys could get the guns and shoot at us if we leave them here. I can't shoot this thing!" Karen shoved the gun back at Debbie as she loaded two other guns.

Debbie finished loading the guns, "Karen, get a grip! We need your help. If Al, Vic and Augie come out first and we need to leave we'll simply take the guns with us, okay." Debbie, Joann, and Phyllis readied themselves for action.

Karen looked at them and then the gun; "I still can't shoot this thing, especially at people!"

Debbie looked over at Karen, "Crouch behind the rock, and put the gun barrel up and ready. You don't have to shoot at people just make noise and point it in the general direction. Karen, just make noise with it, okay?" Debbie waited for a response.

Karen crouched behind the rock and propped the barrel up like she was ready for something. "I'll try to help you. Al said you should take care of me. I don't think he meant put a gun in my hand." Karen gave Debbie a rather indignant look.

Debbie put her hand on Karen's shoulder to reassure her. "I don't like it either but we have to try and get Al, Vic and Augie out of here too. About that moment Debbie thought she heard a whistle behind them. "Did you hear that?"

They all put the guns down and turned around, "What?"

"Shhh…listen." Debbie motioned for Joann, Phyllis and Karen to stay where they were as Debbie walked over to the edge of the water. About that time a motorboat busted through the waterfall and skidded in sideways to the sandy landing spraying water everywhere. Debbie was drenched, shocked and mystified. "Oh!" She cried as she fell back in surprise landing on her behind.

They were all a bit shocked and happy they didn't follow Debbie down to the water. They were still dry! Laughing, David leaped off the boat. "Sorry mom, I didn't expect you to be so close to the water." He held out his hand to help her up. Debbie grabbed David's hand and got up brushing the wet sand from her wet bottom.

All the commotion brought Al, Vic, and Augie running out of the tunnel. They were overjoyed to see David. They ran over to hug him when they noticed Debbie standing there dripping wet. Al raised his eyebrow, "what happened, did you go swimming?"

Debbie was slightly indignant, "No, I got to close to the water for David's heroic arrival."

Joann laughed, "Well at least he didn't drive through your house like you did rescuing Phyllis and Augie."

Karen interrupted everyone, "Should we take these guns with us?" She asked holding up one in each hand.

Al was shocked, "Karen, where did you get the guns?" He rushed up to where she was standing and took the guns away from her.

Debbie rushed towards Karen as well to retrieve the guns but when Al got there first Debbie passed them and picked up the other guns. "I got the guns and ammo out of the cellar. I thought we might need them if something happened to you."

Everyone stood there looking at Debbie. They were shocked, "You mean you girls were going to shoot these guns?" Al held the guns up and gestured towards Debbie.

"Yes Al, we were. We were fully aware of how to use them. In an emergency." Debbie walked towards the boat.

Al was upset. "That's just great! Karen doesn't know how to use them."

Debbie stopped and turned around, "Yes she does, I showed her how while you were wasting time in the tunnel." Debbie raised her eyebrows at Al, in fact and proceeded to the boat.

Karen interrupted Al, "Al, I was okay and she did show me how to use one of those guns. I don't think you have anything to be so worked up over. We didn't have to use them did we?" Karen smiled and picked up the ropes, bungee cords and the rest of the ammo.

David, Vic, Joann, Phyllis and Augie were amused at the tempered discussion of the guns. David laughed, "It's okay Al, be thankful nothing happened and let's get going." David helped Karen, Phyllis and Joann into the boat and Augie, Vic, Al and Debbie were more than happy to climb aboard as well.

David started the engine and checked to make sure he was clear of the sand bar. Al realized David was going to take the boat back through the waterfall. "David, will we all get wet?"

Debbie snickered, "Afraid of a little water, Al?" Debbie collected all the guns and ammo and shoved them up under the canopy, then sat down in the back of the boat and smiled up at Al.

Al grumbled, "No, I'm not afraid of a little water. I just happen to prefer staying dry. Thank you." Al moved to the front of the boat under the canopy and Karen, Joann, Phyllis, Augie and Vic joined him.

Joann looked back at Debbie. "I guess if you're already wet it doesn't matter if you get wet again, uh, Debbie?" Joann asked with a chuckle.

Debbie laughed, "No, it doesn't matter at all. Are you guys crowded? Hang on!" David turned the boat and gunned it. Off they flew, right through the waterfall.

David gunned it before everyone could hang on and Al was thrown right out the back of the boat. While Joann, Vic and Karen landed in Debbie's lap practically. Debbie was amazed, she didn't even get all that wet. Augie and Phyllis managed to be hanging on when David gunned the boat.

They were all laughing and collecting themselves when David asked, "Where did Al go?"

Joann, Vic, Karen and Debbie tried to contain themselves as they looked around and couldn't see Al. "Oh no!" Karen exclaimed. "He's gone."

Debbie laughed, "No such luck." She pointed towards the waterfall and out swam Al. "I guess you have to hang on if you don't want to go for a swim, Al." They were still giggling and carrying on as they helped Al on board.

Karen put her arms around Al in concern. "Are you okay, Al?"

Al grumbled, "Yes, I'm okay, just wet thank you."

Debbie giggled at Al, "I guess you won't have to worry about the water now, will you Al."

Phyllis and Augie were amused. "I find it interesting that David drives his boat much like his mother drives her car."

Debbie frowned for a moment and then smiled. "I think David did a great job in rescuing us."

Once they came out of the waterfall David took the boat back around the island to the dock in front of the cabin. David maneuvered the boat into an inlet that had a covered boat garage and they waited on the boat. They were all confused. Debbie was concerned, "Was it you I saw this morning coming to the island?"

David sat down and turned the engine off. "Yes, mom, it was dad, Bob and I. I guess you panicked when you saw Bob, he was the first one off the boat."

Debbie shook her head, "I didn't expect you back so soon. And I didn't expect you to have someone with you. It's always been just you and dad."

David put his arm around his mother's shoulder. "It's okay, you did good and everyone is safe. When I found out where you were I took dad and Bob back to the marina to pick up everyone and Stony Bottom."

Joann, Vic, Augie, Phyllis, Al and Karen were not sure about this news, "Stony Bottom? Everyone?"

Al was a little up set, "What do you mean everyone and who is Stony Bottom? What about the agents that want to kill us?" Al was going into overload, "I can't believe you would bring everyone out here and put us all in danger again. And why are we just sitting here?"

David took Al over and sat him down on a bench. "Don't panic Al. Everything is okay. The agents that kidnapped you are in jail and Director Daniels has confessed and is in jail as well. The trial is a few weeks away so you don't have to worry anymore. We are safe for right now. I thought it would be a good time to get the maps together and do a little treasure hunting. I thought it would be fun for all of us to pitch in and find out what the fuss is all about. What do you think Al?" David looked expectantly at Al for a response.

Al looked at David, "Oh, I don't know. The map has been nothing but trouble since I found it. And Dave and Debbie found the second map. I guess if they are willing to share it then I'll share too. There's just one thing I want to know, who is Stony Bottom, and why do we have to share with him?" Al stood up and crossed his arms.

Debbie began to laugh, "You think Stony Bottom is a person? Don't you think the name is rather stupid?"

Al looked over at Debbie, "Yes, I do think the name is stupid, so who is it?"

Debbie began to laugh again and David joined her. Everyone was interested in who this Stony Bottom was. David looked at all their inquisitive faces, "Stony Bottom is the name of my scavenger boat. I keep it anchored over at the marina. I like to go diving in this lake. It's an amazing and interesting lake to explore."

Karen perked up, "Oh how interesting, we get to go diving!" She clapped her hands in delight.

Al looked stunned, "No Karen, we don't get to go diving. Are you nuts? Diving is for people who know what they are doing. Besides the map… the treasure, we think, is on land…isn't it?" Al looked suddenly worried.

Debbie was proud to announce, "No, Al, the map indicates the treasure or whatever it is we are to find is somewhere in this lake. I guess you're primed for another swim!" Debbie giggled and Joann joined her.

Al walked over to David, "You mean the boat is so we can go diving for real? They aren't just coming to join us on this island. Land!"

David looked at Al, "No, we think it's in the lake. Dad and everyone are coming to pick us up. Oh look, they are here now!" Saved by the arrival of the boat David quickly started the engine and circled his boat around the large scavenger boat so he could launch it up on the back of Stony Bottom. David had fixed up the scavenger boat with a launch dock for his high-speed motorboat.

When David engaged the engine he headed straight for the back of the scavenger boat. Al, Vic and Joann got excited. "Hang on!" David suggested. He drove it straight onto the back quickly shutting down the engine. A ramp lifted the boat out of the water turning sideways to the back of the scavenger boat and delivering them to the boat deck.

Al, Vic and Joann were wide eyed. Karen sat there smiling. "Oh that was fun, David. What made you think of it?" Karen asked. Al, Vic and Joann were speechless.

David smiled and hopped off the boat onto the deck of Stony Bottom. "I decided I needed a launch for my speed boat so with the help of Dusty, we engineered the back of Stony Bottom to do just what I wanted. It will launch the speed boat as well." David helped everyone off onto the deck where Dave and their friends were waiting.

Bob stepped forward and hugged David "Nice pair of boats you have son."

David smiled, "Thanks Bob, I'm glad I finally get a chance to show them to you. How is Donna holding up?"

Dave walked up, "She's nervous as usual, but Debbie went in to make sure she's okay. Don't worry."

David hugged his dad, "I'm going to see how she is. Have everyone meet in the main cabin and we'll get started examining the maps and discussing our next plan of action. I have to talk to Dusty and Terri as well. They are driving this boat to our next location." David took off to see Donna and his mom. Dave, Bob and Al got everyone into the main cabin for their meeting. They were all eager to see the maps that had been found.

David knocked on the door of Donna's cabin. "Hey Donna, are you okay?"

Debbie opened the door, "Come on in, she's resting."

David entered the cabin as Debbie shut the door. David hugged his mother. "Mom," David sat down and looked at his mother. "We are all meeting in the main cabin to examine the maps. Before we do I have to discuss the second map with you."

Donna looked at David's face he was very serious. "Is something wrong, David?"

David put his hand on Donna's arm, "No I don't think anything is wrong but only mom can answer that question. How did you find the second map? It was just a theory of Dads. He asked you to look in the cave at the symbol he thought was the same symbol that was on the map. Dad never in his wildest dreams thought you would come up with another map. How did that happen? Dad thought the first map was leading us to the symbol in the cave at Trepid Falls. A theory that perhaps it was a clue and the cave was where to start looking for the treasure." There was a knock on the door. Debbie walked over and opened the door it was Dave. "Come in dad, we just started talking about the second map."

Dave, David and Donna looked at Debbie for an explanation. "Joann and I went to Trepid Falls because you asked me to go take a look at the symbol. It was the same symbol that was on the map I had. I also looked the symbol up in a book I had at the library. The symbol is a sacred symbol of several Native American tribes in the western half of the US. I remembered some legends and other stories of myth and mystery about the southwest. Stories of lost Spanish treasures, and lost Dutchman treasures, one in the same I believe. When I was in the cave I found more than the map, I found a journal. It wasn't laying out so I could just stumble onto it. It was hidden beyond the symbol. As I studied the area around the symbol I wasn't sure what I was supposed to find. I know Dave told me to just check out the symbols to see if they were the same. Once I had done that something kept nagging me to look further.

All the silly legends and stories of lost treasure and lost people surrounding the treasure kept clouding my mind. It was as if something was telling me to look further. Haven't you ever had that happen?" Debbie began to pace, "You know that small voice that keeps telling you, you are missing something." She looked at Dave, David and Donna. Debbie continued, "I sat on the floor of that cold damp cave staring at the symbol for hours. I even forgot Joann was outside keeping watch and waiting. I don't know why but I got my pocketknife out and started carving out the piece in the middle of the symbol. To me it was just a rock, but then I gouged it pretty good with my knife and discovered it to be a good sized piece of turquoise."

David interrupted, "How big?"

Debbie sat down, "About nine inches long and every bit of six inches around. I dug it out and discovered a book behind it, a journal. I thumbed through the pages in fascination and in the back was another map like the first one but the leather was different, well you know I showed you the map. I replaced the rock with another rock about the same size but wider. I had a zip lock bag with me so I put the journal in it took the rock and joined Joann. It was dark so Joann didn't know I had anything but a key to the map, or so she thought. The rest of the story you know pretty much."

David thought for a minute, "Where are the journal and rock now?"

Debbie sighed, "The rock is in a compartment under the seat of my car. The journal and map are in my bag."

Dave clasped his hands together, "Good now maybe we can get back to the main cabin and join the group to plan what to do."

David looked at his dad. "Aren't you the least interested in what was in the journal and who wrote it? After all the second map was found in the journal."

Dave had opened the door, looking back at Debbie, David and Donna, he commented, "I believe Debbie is about to share that information with everyone of us." Dave smiled, "Come on let's go share."

Debbie promptly went out the door; David helped Donna up and then down to the main cabin where they were all meeting

# CHAPTER 17

Al looked at all his friends smiling faces and eager readiness to get started finding the treasure or whatever the map would lead them too. He watched as they all laughed and hugged each other. Thinking to himself Al wondered about everyone who was there "Vic and Joann, always eager for adventure. Marlene and Gene, Gene had to think there was treasure or he probably wouldn't be there. Carol and Harley, always looking for a challenge. Phyllis and Augie, they lost their house thanks to Debbie, they had nowhere else to go. Bob and Donna probably wanted to cheer them on. Harold and Dorothy, probably just wanted something to do. Pastor Gerry and Norma, yes we need prayer and spiritual guidance when we find what's at the end of the map. Cindy? What's she doing here? Tired of waiting tables I guess. Archie and Maxine? Archie sold him out to the bad agents, what's he doing here!

Al felt a frown come over his face. He was getting mad, and then he spotted Glenn! Glenn, he doesn't do anything unless he spends hours planning. With Debbie involved there certainly wasn't any planning going on. How could Glenn stand it, no planning? This was more spontaneity going on then even Al could handle so how in the world could

Glenn handle it?

Al shook his head, and then he heard David's voice, "Al! Are you coming?" David held the door open for Al to enter the main cabin.

Al walked in and took a seat at the table, "How do you do it, David?"

Al looked soulfully at David.

David smiled, "What? How do I do what, Al?"

Al sat at the table as Debbie laid both maps out on it. "How do you live without planning?" Debbie gave Al a sideways glance than sat down by Dave.

David laughed, "My life isn't always like this. I plan when I can. I was raised to think on my feet. That's what makes a good agent. Sometimes you have to go with the flow, wherever it takes you." David patted Al on the shoulder. "Don't worry, mom is very good at thinking on her feet. Dad too, after all they taught me to do it."

Al smiled, "You're so reassuring. What on earth is Glenn doing with a bunch of people that haven't planned or know what they are doing next?"

David looked over at Glenn who was talking with Harley and Bob; they looked like they were having a good time. "Glenn is having the time of his life, and so are you. Come on let's just examine these maps."

Bob looked around at everyone sitting at the table. "Who's driving this tub?"

Dave looked up from the table, "Dusty, Terri and Dusty joined us. Terri's one of the best divers around and we thought it would be good to have an experience diver with us, besides David."

Gene looked at David, "You're a jack of all trades aren't you David."

David folded his hands, "Yes, Terri and I have done several dives together. She taught me all I know." David laughed, "Dusty is a pretty good diver too."

Harley chimed in, "That's good I was afraid we would have to go diving. And I don't think that would be good." He shook his head.

Al was amazed; "Some planning has gone into this then. I was thinking we were just flying by the seat of our pants!" Al was relieved.

Bob chuckled, "We are!"

Debbie was anxious, "Are we going to study the maps or just talk about it?"

Glenn piped up, "No we are going to think on our feet!"

Debbie frowned, "Very funny, Glenn."

David pointed to a mark on the map. "I think we need to start here at Pilot cove. I know it's rather remote but I was diving there this spring and there are some underwater caves that look like this mark." David pointed to a mark that looked like a honeycomb. "I thought this would be a good place to start looking. What do you think?"

Al studied both maps, "These maps are the same map. One has Native American signs and the other has early engineering signs. I see what you were talking about now, Dave. This is fascinating to see how they worked together on these maps." Al eagerly studied them.

Debbie clicked her teeth, "Not so fast Al, they aren't exactly the same." she paused.

David realized she was going to tell them about the journal. "What mom's trying to tell everyone is when she found the map she also found a journal. The map was in the back of the journal."

Debbie frowned a little. "Thanks, David I don't think I was having that much trouble telling them." Debbie looked around at a bewildered but curious bunch of friends. I'll get to the journal in a minute. Let's call this map number one and this map number 2. Number one has more signs on it and was made years before map number two. It looks like both end up here at Canyon Lake but not at the same spot." Debbie pointed to the two different spots. "The shape of the lake isn't even the same. Map 1 shows what looks like Marble Point and Map 2 looks like Pilot Cove." Debbie looked at David. "Did you pick Pilot cove because the map was made at a later date than map 1?"

David looked at his mom, "Yes, I studied map 1 when you were sleeping at my house. I discovered the map was dated 1830. I used my resources and looked up some unpublished history concerning maps and history of that era. I studied map 2 when you met up with us at Heavenly. That map was made in 1850, twenty years later. These maps are amazingly alike but you are right about the differences. I think they are either two different maps leading to two different treasures, or someone moved what they found and made a map of their own." David looked at his mother. "Perhaps the journal could shed some light on what map 2 is all about."

Debbie pulled the journal from her purse. It was still in the zip lock baggie. She removed it from the baggie and gently laid it on the table. Debbie had studied old books in college and knew not only the value of the information the book held but also the value of the book alone. "In the beginning of the book there are some entries in a foreign language. As I thumbed through the book on occasion I found some entries in English. The first one stated that he, the author of the journal had been captured by savages."

Dave stood up and got a bottle of water. "What are the odds of finding two different maps leading to the same treasure?"

Pastor Gerry had just walked into the conversation. "What are the odds of finding two maps?"

Bob shook his head, "I don't know, the odds of finding one map to one treasure are rather out standing. The fact that you found two maps and they are so overwhelmingly alike, now that blows my mind."

Debbie looked at Dave and David, "How did you know to tell me where the second map was?"

Dave laughed, "It was a long shot. I remembered seeing a sign on the map you already had. It reminded me of a sign I saw on the wall of the cave we found when we were swimming at Trepid Falls. That's why I told you to go look. I had hoped you would remember what I was talking about. It looks like you did. Purely a long shot!"

Debbie sat there for a minute thinking. "I used the first map to find the second one. They have to be connected somehow. It couldn't have been a coincidence."

Pastor Gerry was eager to share his ideas, "No, not a coincidence, but divine intervention, Yes." He smiled as he looked around at everyone.

Glenn looked at Pastor Gerry, "No way man. Not like this. God wouldn't do something like this."

Pastor Gerry loved a challenge. "God is so amazing, He can do anything, even this." Pastor Gerry smiled, "Yes!"

Harley looked at Pastor Gerry, "Okay, I'll bite. How come God would give us two maps leading to two treasures? Have we been that good?"

Harley laughed.

Glenn spoke up, "It doesn't matter about being good. God isn't going to just up and give us two treasures. Life is crappy and God doesn't give us anything."

Debbie touched Dave's arm, concerned about Glenn's negative attitude. Dave put his hand on Debbie's hand, "Glenn, that's not true and I think you used to know the truth, but gave up on it."

Glenn glared at Dave, "Life's crappy Dave and I don't want to talk about politics or religion, and that's final!"

Pastor Gerry motioned to Dave to let up. "Glenn!" Pastor Gerry said firmly, "We are talking about God not religion. There's a difference."

Glenn looked firmly at Pastor Gerry and Dave, "I don't care I don't want to talk about it."

Al looked at Glenn, "Why are you afraid you might start believing again?"

Glenn got upset, "That's it!" He got up and went out on deck. "Oh great! I forgot I was on a boat, and now I can't leave!" He grumbled under his breath.

Al sat there for a moment, "I like the idea God gave us both maps. Whatever is at the end is a blessing from Him."

Pastor Gerry smiled, "That's a good way to look at it Al."

Glenn came back in the cabin.

Dave and David settled back down into studying the maps. "I think we should continue to look at map two for now. We are already headed to Pilot Cove so I think it's our best plan of action." Dave suggested.

Everyone agreed Pilot Cove first.

The time seemed to pass quickly as they discussed who would dive and which area they would explore first. David pointed to a spot on the Canyon Lake map he happened to have, "This place is honeycombed under the water. I think we should start there."

Debbie tapped her fingers on the table. "Why? Isn't that the place you have been diving with Terri and Dusty?" She asked.

David smiled, "Yes, I have a feeling about the place and we have explored most of the caves there so it won't be hard to eliminate the ones we have already explored." David continued to examine the marine maps he had on hand.

Debbie was restless, "What if the treasure or whatever these maps lead us to isn't here in this lake? Did you think it might not be in the lake, but perhaps back at Trepid Falls or someplace else?" Debbie studied David and Dave.

Dave and David looked at the maps. Al studied the two maps as well and so did most of the people in the cabin of the boat. Al perked up, "You know, Debbie could be right. Look at the newest map; the honeycomb symbol isn't on it. There are two peaks and a stream looking line between them. Right next to the stream is a symbol. Is it familiar to anyone?" Al looked around.

Debbie looked up, "Yes, it is familiar to me." Everyone looked at Debbie inquisitively, as she bit her lower lip. "I saw it in the cave at Trepid Falls when I was looking around the cave."

David chuckled, "No, mom, I don't think anyone would hide their map in the same place the treasure was." David continued to shake his head. "No, no way!"

Debbie laid the journal she had found the map in down and opened it up to a passage written in 1851. "This could shed some light on the examination of the map as well as why he might have hid the map so close to the treasure. Note this paragraph."

Debbie pointed to the paragraph in the journal, it read like this; "It has been what feels like days I have been in captivity. The savages that have held me in this cave will not leave me here. I fear for my life and now I know my life is my greatest treasure. No treasure is worth trading your life for. I fear the savages will return soon and take me away. If anyone finds this journal beware, this cave holds the secrets to a treasure of bounty. Do not risk your life for it. I have risked mine and it wasn't worth it." Debbie closed the journal and picked it up. "That was the last entry in the journal."

David scowled, "The cave holds the secrets to a treasure. It didn't say there was a treasure."

Debbie thumbed through the delicate pages of the journal. "No but the symbols that are through out this journal, I saw in the cave. The man wrote the journal, drew all the symbols in this book and then made that map with them adding some of his own codes or symbols."

Dave gently took the journal as Debbie handed it to him. "He could have done the journal first and then the map or each time he made an entry in the journal he drew a symbol. This is a fascinating find!" Dave said as he closed the book and held it up slightly in gesture.

Al stood staring at the maps. "He knows where the treasure is." He looked up at Dave. "I'm telling you the man who wrote the journal and perhaps fashioned the map saw the treasure!" Al was getting hyped over the idea of treasure. He moved the map he had found at his mothers and placed it aside. "Look." Al pointed to three swirls placed in the middle of the journal map. That looked like three sun signs. "Everything on this map points to the three suns." Al was excited and drawing the attention of everyone in the room. "Debbie, how did you find this journal and map?"

Debbie looked up at Dave and David, "I uh," she stammered.

David jumped in. "Why does that matter Al?"

"It isn't so important how she found it but, man what a find!" Al was so excited at the hope for treasure he was completely disregarding his own map.

David was concerned, "Al, we need to keep in mind both maps. They are both a good find and will assist us in finding what they are both about."

Al shook his head. "I know, but it feels like this map from the journal is so much more direct to where the treasure is."

Dave joined in, "Don't let the map fool you. It isn't clear at all. We have to examine both maps and research the symbols to get anywhere with them.

Terri entered the cabin. "We are at the dive spot and Dusty sent me to tell you. David, are you going to dive with us?"

David collected his thoughts and grabbed the marine map he made some entries on. "Yes I am I'll be there in a second."

"Is anyone else diving with us? Mom, are you going?" Terri inquired.

Debbie smiled a nervous smile, "Do you mind if I go with them Dave?"

Dave hugged her, "No just be careful." Debbie smiled and left to prepare to dive.

Most everyone was surprised. "Debbie dives?" Questioned Al.

Dave patted Al's shoulder, "yes she does and has for sometime. Debbie's been diving with the kids for several years now. Does anyone else want to go with them?" Dave looked around at everyone.

"I think we are all pretty content to stay on board and wait." Bob commented.

Harley and the others agreed to just wait. They all exited the cabin to watch Terri, Dusty, David and Debbie dive into the water. Vic walked up to Dave as they watched the last one dive into the water. "I bet I know why you don't dive, ha Dave." Vic chuckled a little.

Dave laughed, "And I bet you are so right. I am not about to go swimming in cold water let alone dive into it."

Joann walked over to Dave and Vic. "This is one place I don't even want to follow Debbie. I thought she was crazy before, now I know she is." They all laughed.

As time passed and the divers were gone Dave and some of the other guys walked the deck of the boat and watched for unwelcome company and anything else out of the ordinary.

## CHAPTER 18

*As plans* go, many times they change. This was one of those times. David, Dusty, Terri and Debbie had been diving for two hours and had not surfaced. Dave and all the others were getting concerned. "Worried about the length of dive time?" Bill asked Dave. "How long can they dive at one time?"

Dave thought for a minute. "I think the tanks were two hour tanks."

Vic was concerned; "It's been two hours plus by now fifteen or twenty minutes more. Something is wrong."

Dave looked at the water for a sign of someone returning. He walked around the boat looking. "If something is wrong it wouldn't be all four of them. Someone would surface and let us know." Dave twisted his face. "Don't you think?" By now he wasn't sure of much.

Harley walked back and forth from one side of the boat to the other looking for them to resurface. He stopped by Dave. "No, I don't think something would happen to all four of them. They must have found something and for some reason unknown to us, they stopped to check it out."

Pastor Gerry patted Dave's back. "Don't worry, I think they are okay or one of them would return."

Dave smiled a strained smile. "I think you're right."

Phyllis, Carol and Augie came rushing up to Dave and Harley. "Look there's a boat approaching us." They were a little excited.

"What do you think they want?" Carol questioned.

Dave and Harley looked across the lake. Vic joined them with some field glasses to have a look. "It appears to be Forest Rangers. Here take a look." Vic handed the glasses to Dave.

By now everyone had gathered on the deck of the boat. Dave studied the boat that was approaching rather rapidly. "They're going rather fast." Dave commented. "However they do appear to look like Rangers." Dave quickly told everyone to stay calm. Then he motioned Harley and Vic to follow him.

Gene and Pastor Gerry stopped him. "What are you planning on doing?" Gene inquired.

Dave stopped for a second and glanced back at the approaching boat. "I'm not sure. The Rangers could be legitimately checking us out or all the questionable characters that have been chasing some of us are not captured yet. I'm beginning to think there is a deep pool of questionable characters and my wife and kids could be in trouble." Dave looked around at everyone and then at Vic. "There is only one reason I would swim in cold water, and this is one of those times." Then he singled Pastor Gerry out. "Pastor Gerry, could you start preaching and have everyone gathered for it?"

Pastor Gerry smiled. "I sure can! Get everyone seated for the teaching of the year Gene and hurry!" Gene quickly gathered everyone up and told them to help make it good.

Glenn panicked and went rushing off to find Dave, Harley and Vic. "Dave!" Glenn yelled. "I'm coming with you!"

Dave, Harley and Vic looked up from the swim platform. "We're diving Glenn, I'm not sure you can handle it." Dave was reluctant to let Glenn come with them. "I don't think there's a wet suit."

Glenn looked overheated and red in the face. "I'll be okay, I can stand the cold better than you. Please let me come. I don't want to stay and listen to a sermon."

"Oh Glenn, I don't think a teaching will hurt you, it could do you some good." Dave finished putting on his wet suit and was in a hurry to dive.

Glenn pleaded! "Please!"

Dave was reluctant but agreed to let him go. "Okay Glenn, but you have to keep up, I don't want to worry about you too.

Glenn eagerly jumped down on the swim platform and grabbed some diving gear.

Gene rushed over, "They're pulling up beside us, Dave. You guys need to disappear just incase they are after the map.

Dave acknowledged Gene's advice and checked everyone's gear. "Let's go." Dave, Harley, Vic and Glenn all slipped into the water. Dave waved his hand at Gene to let him know they were okay to go.

Slowly the four men floated down the side of the boat staying real close to it. "My it's cold in this lake." Vic stammered as he shivered from the cold water.

Dave was shivering as well. "Yes, these wet suits don't help much." They heard the boat engine turn off. Dave looked at Harley, Vic and Glenn holding his hand to his mouth to quiet them. "Don't speak." Dave whispered, "We may need to dive so make sure you go quietly."

The men bobbed up and down listening to what was happening on deck. Pastor Gerry was preaching what sounded like one of his best teachings yet. Glenn bobbed up and down with a strained look on his face. He couldn't go up or down. There was no hiding or escaping from all Gods truths Pastor Gerry was expounding on. Dave, Harley and Vic looked at Glenn and just smiled.

About that time Pastor Gerry stopped preaching. They could hear Gene, "Can we help you?" Gene inquired of the men in the other boat. It was silent for a moment.

"Where's the owner of this boat?" A man asked.

Gene spoke up. "What makes you think I'm not the owner of the boat?" he asked.

The man studied the group standing beside and behind Gene. "Because I know the owner of this boat. He is out on this lake several times a month."

Gene and the man studied each other. "If you know that then you should know his name shouldn't you?" Gene was pressing the man.

The man started to board David's boat. Gene, Pastor Gerry, Augie, Bob, Harold, and the others stepped forward. "Just a minute sir, you were not invited to board this vessel." Gene stated.

The man stepped back. "Where is the owner of this boat?" He shouted this time.

Pastor Gerry held up his hands as if to hush the man. "Some of our friends had to go to the bathroom so he took the dingy and they went to shore. What is the problem? Can we help you?" Pastor Gerry asked.

The man and his companions looked around and studied the shoreline. "I don't see his dingy, and you are in a restricted area." He continued to study the group of people.

"What makes you think we are in a restricted area?" Asked Bob in his ever so quiet, humble manner.

The man was agitated, "The restrictions in this area are no fishing, or motor boats. You fall into those two categories."

Dave, Harley, Vic and Glenn had heard enough. "Come on let's dive." Dave whispered. "I think Gene and the others can handle this situation." Dave pushed himself down under the water and the others followed. Glenn pushed himself and popped right back up. He did this twice. Then Dave, Harley and Vic grabbed him and pulled him under. Glenn was shook for a moment but gained composure and off they swam to find David, Terri, Dusty and Debbie.

# CHAPTER 19

*Dave, Harley,* Vic and Glenn searched the honeycomb caves for an hour and a half. None of the caves led to anything but a dead end. Discouraged and frustrated they returned to the boat Stony Bottom. Upon approaching the boat Dave noticed the boat that they were approaching wasn't Stony Bottom at all and there was only one boat in sight. He stopped and gathered the others pointing to the boat and with some struggle in the sign language department tried to tell them it wasn't their boat. Dave turned around and headed away from the boat. The others followed. They swam for about ten minutes until Dave spotted some cover. He was hoping they could surface and not be seen. Dave emerged to the surface of the water behind a bunch of fallen timber. Harley, Vic and Glenn followed him. As they came up Dave motioned to them to keep down and quiet.

"What's going on Dave?" Harley asked.

Dave crept out of the water staying behind the brush and timber. As soon as they were all on shore and hidden Dave felt comfortable to talk. "Look at the boat. It's not Stony Bottom."

The other men looked at the boat. "Where did our boat go?" Asked Glenn.

Vic studied the situation. "The guys that were in that boat are waiting for us to return. They must have taken our boat and our friends someplace."

Harley sat down on a log. "Man! I don't want to be stuck wearing this wet suit in public. We need to locate David and the others before they return to the wrong boat. Maybe we should go back into the water and try harder to locate them."

Glenn looked at Harley like he was crazy. "We were looking seriously for them. We looked for over an hour."

Dave felt the tension arise in the men. "David should recognize his own boat or should I say recognize that his boat is replaced with the wrong boat. I'm sure if I can discern there's a problem he can too. After all he's been doing this kind of work more than I have." Dave sat down on a log beside Harley.

Vic looked at the boat again. "What if David doesn't realize the boat isn't his? We knew something could be wrong, David left us thinking everything was alright."

Glenn found a log to sit on too. "I say we wait. David is sure to surface and hopefully he will realize the problem before he climbs on board."

Dave looked at his watch; "We didn't go diving to look for them until they had been gone at least two and a half hours. We were gone looking for another hour and a half or so. They have been gone for four hours or more. I am getting worried and we only have a couple hours left of good light. I don't know what to do anymore." Dave shook his head in frustration.

Glenn tried to lighten the situation. "Man just think, four plus hours in water. They must be extremely wrinkled by now." The men gave Glenn a sick look. "What? I'm just trying to help lighten us up."

Harley got up and walked over to look out at the lake and boat. "Dave! Come here quick."

Dave rushed over to Harley and looked out at the boat. There was a head bobbing up and down towards the end of the boat. "I better go and see if it's David." He grabbed his tank and gear and crept back towards the water.

Vic followed him. "Wait I'll go with you. You guys wait here."

Dave didn't say a thing he just fixed his gear and slipped into the water with Vic close behind. Harley and Glenn watched the boat and the surfaced head. About that time another head popped up. Harley got nervous. "I hope you and I don't have to rescue anyone. I don't think I could come up with a good plan."

Glenn just watched as another head popped up. "Now there are three. What do we do if Dave doesn't get there in time to stop them?"

Harley shook his head, "I think they know by now the boat isn't David's boat. They may think we are all prisoners though."

Glenn grabbed Harleys arm. "The majority of the guys are their prisoners. What else could have happened to them?" Glenn walked back to his log and sat down. "Oh no, poor Al and Karen. They are being held prisoner again."

Harley looked back at Glenn and frowned. "Come on Glenn, snap out of it. They won't be for long." He looked back at the boat. "There are six heads bobbing up and down. I think Dave and Vic got there." Harley turned around and sat down in relief.

It wasn't long when Dave returned with Vic, David, Terri, Dusty and Debbie. Harley and Glenn were glad to see them but tried to remain quiet and calm. "Are we glad to see you!" Glenn announced as quietly and casual as he could, "Where have you been?"

Harley studied the boat for a moment and then joined the conversation. "I am sure glad to see you too but perhaps we should try to figure out why the guys on the boat look like they are preparing to dive."

Dave, David and the others rushed over to take a look through the bushes. David studied them closely. "I think that's Dante, he was supposed to be picked up along with the Director and other agents of question. I guess they didn't catch up with him." David kept watching what they were doing.

Dave turned and sat down. "Do you think he has been watching you for awhile, David?"

David glanced back at his dad, "Perhaps he has been watching me. I know he has been giving me plenty of grief lately. However I turned him into the internal affairs office along with the other agents and the Director."

Dusty put his arm around Terri as she was shivering. "I think he's either a smooth talker or the internal affairs officers haven't caught up with him yet. I would be careful David until you can be sure of who you can trust."

Dave rested his arms on his knees, "If we can't trust anyone we are out here on our own. We also need to think about your boat David, and the other friends we have left on it."

David turned away from watching the boat and leaned on the tree. "I pray the agency isn't all bad. I have to believe..."

About that time Harley interrupted, "Dave, David!" He almost shouted but caught himself and slid it down to a whisper. "Look, if I didn't know better I would say Gene, Marlene, Pastor Gerry and Norma were on board that boat with your Dante fellow."

David and Dave got up and looked, as did everyone else. They couldn't believe their eyes. Terri shook her head. "We do know better, look closely at them. They favor our Gene, Marlene, Pastor Gerry and Norma but look at their demeanor."

Debbie watched as they moved around on the boat. "Are they using those people to make us think our friends are on that boat and maybe we'll surface?"

Dave noticed the fellow that favored Pastor Gerry was smoking. "I see what you mean Terri. Pastor Gerry would never smoke. The likeness is astounding."

What do you think we should do? Asked Vic.

David watched for a minute longer. "They just sent two divers into the water. I think we need to get out of here."

Glenn looked astonished at David. "Why?"

David gathered his gear. "We need to find our friends and it is apparent they think we are somewhere around here. It won't take them long to find us." David studied the situation.

All the others started gathering their gear. Dave walked over to David and Vic joined them. "Do you think we should start hiking off to the south west until we get to another place at the lake we can dive?" Dave asked David.

David pulled a map of the lake from his pack and spread it out on the ground. They all took a look at the map. "I don't think it will take to long to get over here at the cliffs. We would have cover from the boat.

How much time does everyone have on their tanks?"

Dave checked his meter. "I have about thirty minutes left and so should Harley, Vic and Glenn. Do you guys have thirty minutes?" Dave asked them.

Harley, Vic and Glenn checked their meters commented they had thirty minutes or about that on their tanks. Glenn spoke up, "Do you guys have about that much time on your tanks?" he asked David.

David smiled, "no we have forty five minutes on ours." David pulled his tank up and put it on his back.

Glenn looked skeptical. "You were gone more than two hours while we worried about you on the boat. Why aren't your tanks empty?"

David laughed, "we weren't under water the whole time, that's why!"

Dave, Vic, Harley and Glenn all shared the surprise. "Where were you?" Asked Vic.

Debbie smiled that ever so cleaver smile, "We were treasure hunting!"

She then nodded her head at them.

David interjected, "We can talk about this later. Right now we need to get across this wooded area to the lake and back to the marina before these guys on the boat decide to return. Shall we go?" David started off in the general direction and everyone followed.

## CHAPTER 20

*It took* longer than David and Dave thought it would take to reach the cliffs at the lake. The tanks were heavier crossing land and no one had on the appropriate footwear. They arrived tired and sore. By now it was getting dark. They all sat down and unloaded the tanks and other gear they were carrying. David climbed up on the rock cliffs to see if the boat was in the cove. It was gone. He scrambled back down the rocks.

Dave stood up, "what's wrong David?"

David proceeded to paw through his pack and retrieved some binoculars. "The boat is gone. I didn't see it in the cove." He started scanning the lake for the boat. "How long did it take us to cross the land, dad?" David asked.

Dave looked at his watch. Vic and the others looked too. Harley spoke up. "I believe it took about thirty minutes."

Dave studied the lake too. "Do you see them?"

David put his binoculars back in his pack. "Yes, I believe they were just pulling into the marina. I wonder if the others are still on my boat? Make sure you are rested and we will go ahead and swim back to the marina."

Glenn was surprised. "Tonight?"

David glanced at Glenn, "Yes, tonight. We don't have a minute to waste, we have to figure out where our friends are."

Debbie was getting ready. "How long will it take us to swim back to the marina?"

Dave went over to help her put her tank on. "I think at least an hour maybe more. It would be nice if a returning boat picked us up." He then proceeded to put his tank on.

David smiled, as he got ready to dive. "I think you may be right dad. It would be nice and faster if a boat picked us up. We better get started."

Vic was struggling a little with his gear so David helped him. "I suppose the water is getting colder."

Dave said he hoped not yet. Dusty helped Terri put her tank on and gather her gear. "If we swim fast we might warm up." Dusty chuckled.

"Are we diving or just swimming?" Glenn inquired.

David looked at everyone to see if they were ready to go. "We are going to swim first. If the need arises we will dive. Our air in the tanks is limited and there isn't enough to dive long enough to get back to the marina so we have to swim most of the way. If we conserve now we will have enough to dive and swim into the marina unnoticed. Let's go!" David turned and entered the lake, the others followed. "Stay close together." David instructed.

The water was cold and the swim was a difficult one. Unfortunately no boats passed by on their way to the marina. By the time they all arrived to the marina they were extremely cold and not exactly willing to dive for any reason. It was dark and no moon so they had enough cover to swim into the marina area. Slowly and carefully they quietly swam towards the boats and dock. David spotted his boat Stony Bottom. It looked deserted. Dave knew where they could get a shore without much difficulty and not be seen. So he took the lead.

Once on shore everyone removed their tanks and gear. Dave crept through the parking lot to locate his vehicle. David dropped his gear and decided to check out Stony Bottom. "I'll be back in a few minutes. Give me about twenty minutes and if I'm not back leave without me."

Harley wasn't sure that was a good idea. "Wait David, your dad doesn't know you are going to check out your boat. Someone should go with you."

David did not want to wait. "I'll be okay, if there's something a miss I'll give you a signal."

Vic was concerned. "I'll go with you. You sound to much like your mom."

Debbie scowled, "Hey, I do okay for myself. I'm sure he'll be okay too."

Vic insisted so David agreed. "We'll be back in a few minutes." David said again. Off they swam into the dark.

Glenn looked around. "Do you think this Dante guy is waiting for David to do exactly what he is doing?"

Dusty walked to the edge of the water and looked toward the boats. "I do, he apparently has been a few jumps ahead of us all day. If you feel up to it Harley why don't you and I follow David and Vic just to keep an eye on their backs."

Harley agreed. "Wait" Debbie suggested. "What if something should happen to all four of you?"

Dusty hugged Terri. "Don't worry we won't get to close." Dusty and Harley slipped into the cold water and disappeared into the dark.

About that time Dave came back. "Where are David, Vic, Harley, and Dusty?" He asked.

Glenn was beside himself. "They all went to check out David's boat. I guess they think there's a chance the others are still on the boat."

"Where's the car, Dave." Debbie whispered.

Dave sat down. "I didn't get it. There were several people walking around and some in vehicles. I couldn't tell if they were with Dante or not, so I just looked around and came back."

Debbie sat down by Dave. "What now?" she asked.

Dave watched the marina. "We wait for David and the others to come back. Not much else we can do."

Terri was shivering. "I'm so cold dad. Is there a chance you could get some blankets or coats from the car?"

"No, sorry. It's to risky, just sit close to mom, maybe if we stay close together it will help." Dave put his arms around Terri and Debbie. Glenn sat close by them too. They were so quiet you could hear them breathing. Not one said a thing.

## CHAPTER 21

David and Vic slowly and quietly approached the boat Stony Bottom. Right next to it was Dante's boat. "What do you think?" Whispered Vic.

David and Vic slowly moved through the water until they were between the boats. "Shh" David motioned with his hand for Vic to climb the ladder. Vic climbed to the top of the dock. Upon approach he was careful to check out the dock for movement or anything else out of the ordinary. Then he climbed on top and motioned to David. David climbed up to where Vic was. They both slipped into the dark shadows. David studied the boat looking for someone hiding in the shadows.

Vic noticed someone in the shadows of the other boat. He tugged on David's arm. "Look, someone in the shadow." Vic whispered. He could scarcely breath trying to be so quiet.

David looked at the other boat. "You're right." Looking around for a retreat, he motioned to Vic to climb down the other side that was still in the dark shadows. Vic moved back and climbed down on the other side of the dock. David watched the man in the shadows of Dante's boat. The man moved out of the shadows toward the dock and looked toward David. Vic was waiting for David to climb down. Looking up he could see the back of David. Vic realized there was something happening. He climbed back up and peaked over the dock. Knowing David couldn't move Vic climbed back down.

As Vic waited for David he heard movement in the water. He looked around but couldn't see much of anything, as it was quite dark. The sound came from the direction of David's boat Stony Bottom. Vic decided to move further down the ladder until he was half way into the water. Leaning way over Vic tried to see what was making the sound. As the water glistened in what little light reflected from the buildings on shore, Vic noticed something in the water. He carefully lowered himself down into the water and a dark shadow. Slowly he moved to the other side of the dock where he could see the man on Dante's boat as well as check out what was in the water with him. As he floated into position he saw the man on the boat leave and disappear into the cabin of the boat. Vic looked back to see if David was coming. Sure enough, David climbed down the ladder. Vic whispered, "David, I'm over here." About that time there was a splash. Vic and David about jumped out of their skin.

Looking around David noticed something bobbing up and down in the water. He then glanced over to the side of his boat to see something drop into the water. "Vic, I think our friends are escaping on their own." David floated over to Vic. "Do you see any more movement on Dante's boat?" He whispered.

Vic looked up at the boat. "No not yet, but if they keep splashing there will be movement on the dock and both boats." Vic was nervous.

David patted Vic's shoulder. "Keep watch I'll help these guys get out of here and back to where mom and dad are." David was trying to keep things under control and quiet. He floated out to help the others and let them know they weren't alone.

Vic heard something behind them. He strained to see in the dark and noticed something in the water back where they had came from. Unsure of what was going on. Vic held his post but managed to get David's attention and let him know there was someone else in the water the way they would be going. David helped the rest of the people out of the boat and had them try to be quiet. It was cold water and so they were all having some trouble keeping quiet. David managed to move them down towards where Dave and Debbie were.

On the way they met up with Harley and Dusty. David was trying to keep quiet but was getting quite cold by now. "What are you guys doing out here." He said as quietly as he could with his teeth chattering.

Harley's teeth were chattering so bad he couldn't even talk. Dusty was able to answer him. "We thought we better keep watch to make sure nothing happened to you and Vic." Dusty and Harley waited for everyone to pass and then they brought up the back making sure no one got lost or drown in the cold water.

Getting back David helped those out of the water that needed help and those that didn't helped too. Once on dry land and away from the brutes that put them in the predicament everyone started to relax a little.

Dave gathered them around. "We need to go to a safe place and get warm and dry. However before we can do that we need to be patient until David and I can come up with a plan." Dave looked at David. "I have already scouted the vehicles in the parking area and I think some of the men with Dante are watching them."

David thought for a moment. "Remember the ranger when I first came to this marina after the shooting?"

Dave smiled, "yes, Ranger Hank! He offered to help us anytime we needed it."

Debbie interrupted, "excuse me guys but can we really trust this Ranger Hank? We don't even know who he is. Maybe he offered to help knowing we might ask and he's really with Dante. Think about it." She said with reservation.

David put his arm around his mom. "Don't worry about Hank. I checked him out after we left here that day. I found he was not a threat. Trust me." David smiled.

Debbie raised her eyebrows. "You're the expert but if it were me I would be more cautious."

Al spoke up. "If it gets us warm and dry quicker I'm all for it. I've been kidnapped twice and I'm starting to get used to the routine."

Karen looked at Al. "Al! I've been kidnapped twice too and I don't like it much. Of course I do want to get warm and dry as soon as possible too."

Phyllis and Augie were standing close by. Augie laughed quietly. "Phyllis and I have been kidnapped twice now too. I don't want to be taken a third time though. It's hard on the body and mind."

Phyllis added, "At least this time we saved ourselves and didn't have to have a car crash through our front door and almost run us over. Wet and cold are an easy fix too." She chuckled some.

Debbie turned to Dave and David. "It won't be long until they discover our friends have escaped. We need to do something as soon as possible."

David grabbed his gear, "I'm on it mom, see you in a few minutes." David winked at his mom, waved to everyone else then off he went into the darkness.

Carol watched intently, "Why did he go that way up through the forest? He could have gone to the parking lot."

Debbie looked amused at Carol. "They think that Dante's men are watching the parking lot so we can't get our cars. It will alarm them if they are watching and then we will be scattering to get away from them again."

Karen shivered, "I hope David hurries, I'm really cold."

Al looked sad and defeated. "What's wrong Al?" Debbie asked.

"Does this end the treasure hunt? I think maybe we would have been better off if I hadn't found that stupid map." Al just shook his head in frustration.

Glenn walked over shivering. "Glenn!" Joann exclaimed, "You're shivering, I have never seen you shiver!" Joann giggled.

Glenn tried to keep his composure. "I don't think you have ever seen me wet or swimming in a cold lake at night either." Glenn sat down by Al. "Don't loose heart big guy. Finding that map has been the highlight for most of us and the adventure will be with us forever."

Al shook his head in agreement. "You know, Karen and I probably would never have been kidnapped if it hadn't been for that map." Al was feeling like maybe there was some good to all these adventures. "I just don't want anyone to get hurt as a result of our need for excitement."

There was an explosion that knocked most of them off their feet and seats. "What was that?" Dave exclaimed. He scrambled to his feet and ran down to the edge of the lake. Debbie and most everyone else followed him.

"Look!" Shouted Vic, "It looks like David's boat."

Dave grew quickly concerned. "Lets get back out of sight and keep quiet. I think they... uh..." Dave looked at everyone. "I'm not sure but...do you suppose Dante and his men think you are all on board the boat?" Dave grew sick inside.

Al just stood there by the lake watching the boat burn. About that time David came flying by in a bus. Opening the door he jumped out. "Hurry up guys and get in we have to vacate this place quick." He then retreated back into the bus.

Everyone gathered them selves together and rushed over to the bus. "Are we glad to see you. They blew up your boat." Harley explained as he boarded the bus.

Everyone was excited as they climbed on the bus. Dave was the last to get on. Looking worried he sat down behind David. "Do you suppose they think all our friends are still on the boat?" Dave was still feeling a bit sick inside.

David took off yelling, "Hang on!" He turned to his dad and then to the road. "I don't know dad. Perhaps they do. Knowing Dante the way I do, I think it is possible. He means business and won't stop until he gets what he wants. I don't want to mess with him. I called the authorities to tell them they missed some of the men and perhaps women that were causing Mobil Park City citizen's problems. I did happen to mention that Dante was the ringleader and he was dangerous. They knew that already and I found out they had been looking for him for some time. We can't take any chances. I borrowed the bus from Ranger Hank and we are going to change vehicles with him in Heavenly. After that we need to get someplace we can regroup and get some rest. These guys look tired." David kept watching the rearview mirrors for anyone following them. "Dad!" David looked back for a moment. "Do you remember the place we used to go when I was little?"

Dave thought for a moment. "Yes, the cabin up Silver Creek. What about it?" Dave looked back at everyone.

David hesitated looking in the mirrors as Al tapped Dave on the arm. He sat across from Dave in the other front seat. "Dave, are we in danger?"

David glanced back at Al. "I'm not going to lie to you Al. We are in grave danger. The guys who had you on my boat are worse than the ones that kidnapped you to begin with. They either thank they killed everyone on the boat except the four of us who were diving or they know you escaped and will be looking for all of us. The last thing we want is for them to find us." David looked back at Al and then to the mirrors and road again. Still no one was behind them.

Al looked worried. "Maybe we should give them my map. Would that make them leave us alone?"

Dave looked at Al and then at David. David was driving very fast. "No Al, it doesn't matter now. These men don't want anyone around who can identify them to the authorities. We have to work with the authorities to catch them."

Al scratched his head. "Have you got any ideas?"

David rounded a curve in the road and finally Heavenly was in sight. "Yes Al, but I need to work on my ideas and maybe get some input from all of you. We are in this together so we all need to be a part of what happens next." Up ahead of them just about three miles from Heavenly was a turnout where they would be meeting Ranger Hank with another vehicle. David had planned to trade the bus for a limousine there. He approached and sure enough Hank was there. David pulled in behind the limo and stopped. "It's the end of this ride folks. I want everyone to quickly get all your things and get into the limo we need to leave as soon as possible." David opened the door and walked out.

There he found Hank relieved to see them. "Am I glad to see you. I didn't want someone else to stop and ask questions."

David shook Hank's hand. "Thanks for all your help. We appreciate it very much." With that Hank waited for everyone to get off the bus and he left right away. David encouraged them to hurry and get into the limo. As soon as they were in David took off going back the way they came.

Harley grew concerned, as was everyone when they realized David was heading back to the lake. "Where are you going, David? We just came from this direction."

David in his reassuring way told them not to worry as he slowed down and turned off the highway onto a dirt road. "Dad, do you remember where the cabin is?" Dave looked around and back at David. "Are you headed up to Silver Creek?"

"Yep" David replied.

Dave sat forward, "As soon as you cross the creek there should be a jeep trail, turn down that and go for about a mile then stop."

David glanced over at Dave, "Stop?"

"Yes, stop, I need to step out and have a look around so I can remember. There isn't a real road to the cabin. We used to just go cross-country. It's dark so I don't know if I can find it." Dave sat back in his seat and looked out the window watching for the creek.

Bob sat behind Dave. "How far have we come?"

Dave turned around. "I'm not sure, I think about sixty miles is all. Of course we have back tracked a little so it's hard to say."

David drove across the creek and slowed down more. Dave and David looked for the jeep trail. It was hard to find, the trail hadn't been used much if at all. Finally they found the trail. David turned off and looked at his speedometer. Then he continued down the rough narrow hard to find trail. The trail followed the creek. When David's speedometer showed they had gone about a mile he stopped. "I think we've gone a mile, dad, should we wait until first light?"

Dave opened the door of the limo. "I'll take a look around and let you know." Dave stepped out into the dark. Everyone sat in the limo waiting. Finally Dave opened the door and got back in. "I think we need to stay here until it gets lighter. I can't see anything out here it's so dark."

David turned around and looked at everyone stuffed in the back of the limo. "Listen guys, we are going to have to stay here tonight. I know it's uncomfortable for you but at least you are warm and dry now." David smiled and tried to force a chuckle.

Al spoke up, "If we take turns getting out and stretching I think we will make it okay. We can also keep watch." Al felt confident once again.

Donna was not happy with the arrangements. "I don't think I can do this. It's getting stuffy already."

Marlene spoke up, "We can open some windows a little to let fresh air in. Will that help Donna?"

"Yes, I think so. I hope so." Donna still wasn't very happy. Bob sat by her and tried to make her comfortable.

Joann tried to lighten the group's spirits. "This might not be such a good thing for Glenn. He might entertain us again with his dreaming." She laughed. Everyone else laughed too, remembering the last time they all stayed together.

Glenn turned red. "I'm not planning on sleeping while I'm around all of you. I plan on keeping watch, believe it or not I think that is safer." Glenn huffed and got out of the limo. Half the others got out as well to walk around. Those who were left in the limo, stretched out to get some sleep.

# CHAPTER 22

*Dawn didn't* come to early. By the time it was getting light most of the men were out side walking around trying to stay warm and awake. The women were uncomfortable and tired in the limo. Dave was relieved to see the light. He started looking for familiar surroundings so he could find the cabin. It had been years since they had been up to the cabin. Debbie got out of the limo to help Dave.

David started the engine and everyone got into the limo to go. Dave and Debbie studied the mountains and trees. "Has something changed Dave? I can't quite remember this meadow and that mountain is in the wrong place."

Dave looked around and then laughed. "You're right. I think we should have gone off the road on the other side...maybe." He looked puzzled; "Lets go check out the road where we crossed the creek." They got in the limo and told everyone what they intended to do.

They all were so tired and frustrated. "At least you are alive." Debbie told them. "We need to stay positive and strong no matter what our circumstances." They all agreed.

David drove back down the trail to the main road. Once they arrived to the road Dave once again got out and looked up and down the side of the road for another trail. Everyone got out and helped him. Debbie looked around at the landscape and mountains. David found what looked like it could have been a jeep trail at one time. "Let's try this trail dad." David yelled in Dave's direction. Dave, Bob, Harley, Vic and Al all came over to David and looked at the overgrown trail.

Debbie came as well. Looking around at the mountains she said it very well could be the trail. "Let's try it." David said and his dad agreed. They all retreated back into the limo. David drove about a mile up the rough hard to find trail and stopped. Dave once again got out and searched for the trail to the cabin. Once he found it they were off again.

The trail wound around a mountain, over hills, through gullies and thick forests. Finally they came to a cabin sitting amidst the trees. The ride had been extremely rough. By the time they arrived everyone was more than glad to escape from the limo.

Bob got out and turned to help Donna out. "Man that was rough, is this car missing a bottom?"

David laughed, "No, but close. Under the circumstances I think this old limo did quite well."

Dave and Debbie approached the cabin. "I can't believe it's looking so good after all these years." Exclaimed Dave walking up onto the porch.

Debbie joined Dave on the porch and they began looking for the key they had hidden so many years ago. "I thought it would be more overgrown than this. You don't think anyone has been here do you Dave?" Debbie asked concerned.

Dave located the key. "No I don't think anyone has been here. We left it pretty clean the last time we were here. It's only been about ten years I think."

David laughed as he walked onto the porch. "You have lost touch with reality dad. It's been fifteen years. The last time we were up here I was twelve."

Dave unlocked and opened the door. "Fifteen years. Really, my how time flies."

Harley entered the cabin. "Not bad for fifteen years. Only a few spider webs and some dirt." He laughed. "Why haven't you been back here? It's not a bad place."

Everyone was coming into the cabin. Al looked around, "Not bad, why has it been so long?"

Dave looked at Debbie for help in answering the questions. "I don't really know." He smiled at Debbie.

Debbie shook off a cushion. "The kids grew up and we seemed to go in a different direction. Our business took off and there wasn't time to enjoy the summers or our cabin. I do miss it, thanks for reminding us about it David." She hugged David.

Everyone was helping to clean up the cabin and collect wood for the night. Donna was exhausted as was Dorothy, Karen, Marlene, Norma, Phyllis and Maxine. Debbie, Joann, Carol and Cindy were preparing something to eat. While the men were sitting around talking, some were sleeping as well as some of the women.

As the day turned into night, everyone had something to eat. They decided who would get the bunks and who would sleep on the chairs and couch. David offered to sleep in the limo and Vic and Harley volunteered to sleep in the limo as well. Dave thought that might be okay as the room in the small cabin was limited.

As Debbie, Joann, Carol and Cindy cleared the table, while others helped wash the dishes. Dave decided it would be a good time for a meeting. David agreed with him. "We need a plan of action now we know who is following us and perhaps looking for us." David went to his pack and retrieved the map. "Get the map and journal mom." David requested.

Debbie gathered her pack and rummaged through it retrieving the map and journal. "Did you want to study them again?" Debbie asked as she approached the table.

"No." David said sternly.

"What then?" Asked Debbie puzzled. Everyone looked at David rather puzzled as well.

David walked over to Debbie and handed her the map he had. "I want you to hold this map and yours. I'll explain in a moment." Then he turned around and went to the sink. Getting a drink of water he returned to the table and sat down.

None of this made since to anyone. Al was next to David, "Where is the map I found at my mothers house?"

David drank some of his water and looked up at Al. "Mom has it now and will be the only one who knows where it is for the moment. Sit down Al, in fact everybody take a chair." David looked at his dad.

Dave always knew when his son was concerned or worried. "Come on folks lets sit and discuss what to do next. What are you thinking David?"

David looked at all the inquisitive faces. "Mom, first and foremost, I want you to hide both maps and the journal. Hide them together or separately it doesn't matter to me just hide them. Do it somewhere in the next twenty four hours." David looked at his mother like she should know what he wanted it was important and serious. Debbie acknowledged David's look with a nod. "Next"

David was interrupted. Al was concerned, "Why can't I take care of my own map? I found it and that should mean something."

David put his hand on Al's arm. "It means you found a very important part of this puzzle and you need to entrust it to mom for now. Dante tried to kill you. It could be because you were with me or because you found something he wants. Right now he may think you are dead, but I'm not going to take that chance. If he manages to get his hands on any one of us, I don't want you to know anymore about the map or maps then you already know. Dante can tell if someone isn't telling the truth. At least I think he could tell if you weren't." David patted Al's shoulder. "What do you know right now?" He looked sternly at Al. "In fact what do any of you know right now?"

They all looked at each other then back at David. "I know I found a map at my mother's in the cellar. I also know they kidnapped me at least once because of it." Al hung his head, "They can be very persuasive, and they made me tell them what I did with the map. So they are after the map. Another point to consider is they didn't answer my question when I asked them how in the world they even knew I had found a map. I think the clerk was in with them and must have listened in on our conversation when I called Dave." Al became demanding. "None of this tells us why you David, and your agents were watching us at Mobil Park City and why you weren't all that surprised when we told you we saw Gene, Marlene, Pastor Gerry and Norma at Canyon Lake Lodge. Your only explanation was that we really didn't see them and you would explain. Isn't this a good time to explain?" Everyone looked at David for an explanation.

David smiled. "Now is a good time for an explanation. Dante is the ringleader for a band of criminals. Descriptions that fit Gene, Marlene, Pastor Gerry and Norma were given in many major crimes that have been committed. Always leading back to Dante of course. About two months ago, probably two weeks before you found the map, Al. Our sources informed us that something was to happen in Mobil Park City. It immediately pointed to Gene and company." David paused.

Marlene was excited, "You don't suspect us do you?"

Gene put his arm around Marlene to calm her. "No." Gene was almost to calm. "David doesn't suspect us. However you knew they would hope you did. Right?" Gene questioned David.

David stared at Gene for a second. "Actually Gene, we did suspect you. Agents have been watching you for quite some time, over a year to be honest with you. It wasn't until your look a likes showed up at Canyon Lake Lodge and you were still in Mobil Park City that I decided maybe you weren't involved. You have to admit some of your activity has been some what suspicious." David studied Gene.

Pastor Gerry and Norma stepped forward. "I have to say we are not involved in any of this mess." Gerry insisted.

Everyone was stunned over this conversation. Joann huffed, "I figured you must be mixed up in something illegal."

David held up his hand, "Now Joann, don't jump to conclusions."

Vic entered the conversation. "I don't think Gene is mixed up with this bunch of thugs."

Gene thanked Vic, "I'm not mixed up with them. I did give information about some of our fine citizens to your Director though. I didn't realize at the time he was on the wrong side of the law. I hope it wasn't something they used against us." Gene took a long deep breath. "I certainly wouldn't want to hurt anyone here. I only hope you know that. Even you Joann." Gene looked at David. "What now?"

"I guess we'll continue laying out a plan. I think mom and dad, Terri, Dusty, Glenn, Vic, Harley and myself need to continue to stay together and if need be lead Dante and his group away from the rest of you. We are going to continue with the thought that they are of the mind you were on the boat that exploded, so you are dead." David looked around at everyone. "Don't worry you will be able to be a big part of the plan. We need to end Dante's activity by capturing his companions. There should be six of them, maybe seven. I'm not sure right now. I'm hoping Gene will help flush out the rest as soon as we capture his double."

Gene looked surprised. "Isn't that dangerous?" Gene looked for a cigarette in his pockets.

Marlene frowned and smacked his arm. "Relax Gene, you don't smoke anymore."

Gene gazed at Marlene in disgust. "Well maybe this could send me over the edge and I will start again."

Dave had been sitting in the back of the room listening. "David, what do you think we should do? Could Sheriff Archie help us?"

David turned around to look at his dad. "No, sheriff Archie was mixed up with my Director. Dante isn't connected with that bunch. We have been tracking Dante for years. Now I have something he wants, I might be able to finally catch him."

Al perked up. "You mean I helped you?" Al seemed pleased.

David smiled, "Yes Al, you discovered something. Dante will kill to obtain. Don't get comfortable though, I don't want any of you caught by this guy or his associates. They are dangerous. Let's get started, if we make Dante think we have the map he will send someone to collect it."

Vic scratched his head. "Why wouldn't he come to get the map himself?"

David looked at Vic, "He is suspicious and that's the reason the agency hasn't caught him yet. Dante sends out feelers to see if there is a trap. Usually he isn't far behind the gopher though. All of us need to out smart Dante. I've been tracking him for years but you haven't. You don't know what he is capable of." David became worried. He rose from the table and walked over to his dad.

Harley spoke up, "Maybe we don't have the training of an agent, but we do have survivor instincts. Look at these guys; they escaped out of the boat before it blew up. Doesn't that count for something?" Everyone agreed.

David was proud and happy they had all escaped. "Yes it does count, you are still alive and here. I just don't want to risk your lives catching this guy."

Al interrupted, "I found a map and we all went treasure hunting. It became dangerous but we all handled it. The kidnapping, twice for some of us and the blowing up of the boat, who's to say when this guy and his comrades get caught and we finally get to go treasure hunting again it won't be dangerous in some way. We have faced danger and I don't know about you but I am better for the adventure. I faced death and lived so far to realize the exhilaration of the experience. I'm too old to care much anymore. I want to live and enjoy the experience. I don't care if there's treasure or not the real treasure is in the adventure." Al was excited.

Everyone else became excited too. Augie smiled, "Yes, it has been an adventure and a dangerous one at that. Phyllis and I almost got run over by Debbie, even though she was rescuing us. What a rush. Let's get this guy!"

They all agreed and told David not to worry they all understood the dangers and risks of helping. Donna was worried, "What can I do to help. I can't run and I don't think I can take to much excitement."

Bob looked at Donna, "You don't need to help. I don't think you could help with something as dangerous as this."

Donna grumbled, "I can too, if I can climb out a tiny window of a boat into freezing cold water and swim half frozen to shore, watch the very boat I just climbed out of minutes before blow up, I can certainly help." Donna was determined to help and no one could tell her other wise.

David calmed them down. "Listen, everyone will have a job to do and hopefully I can manage to keep all of you safe. I'll inform headquarters of Dante's whereabouts. In the mean time everyone get some sleep we will need it come tomorrow. We have to act fast. Could Harley, Vic, dad, Glenn, Dusty, Terri, and mom stay and help me think up a plan?"

As everyone slept that night David and the few he chose made plans to capture Dante and his band of criminals.

# CHAPTER 23

As the sun peeked up over the mountain the cabin was filled with slumber. From out of the twilight in the corner of the room someone was moaning.

Debbie and Dave woke up. "What is that?" Dave questioned indignantly in a whisper.

Debbie began to giggle softly. "I think its Glenn having one of his dreams."

Dave and Debbie tiptoed across the room quietly skirting around the people on the floor sleeping. They approached Glenn who was gripping his blanket, and making mournful noises. Dave gazed at Glenn in disbelief. "Ah…he's smooching the air!" Dave exclaimed in a loud whisper. Debbie started to laugh and then quieted down quickly. Dave walked to Glenn's feet and kicked his foot.

Glenn woke up abruptly. "What!" He jumped upright in the chair. "Is that any way to wake someone up?"

Dave shook his head; "I did it to save you from more embarrassment. I don't think you will ever live the dreaming down. It happens to often." Dave laughed as he walked off to the table and kitchen area of the cabin. Debbie shook her head and followed Dave giggling.

Glenn looked around, some were sleeping and others were awake trying to figure out what was going on. Joann however noticed another chance to tease Glenn. Dave started waking everyone up so they could get organized and on they're way to executing the plan of attack on Dante. Glenn just ignored Joann.

David had outlined all the ideas and made a print out for everyone. As soon as people were awake and ready they got started unfolding the plan. David handed out the outline of the plan to everyone. "I have outlined what we think might work in finding and capturing Dante." David stated. "Examine the outline and we will discuss it in a moment." David sat down at the table and examined the document too.

After a few minutes Dave and almost everyone was finished reading what they intended to do. David stood up. "Are there any questions?" He asked. They all looked up at David and agreed collectively that it looked good.

Donna just had to ask her question. "What if we're in the middle of doing something and the plan blows up in our faces?"

David smiled, "Don't worry, I think the key positions will be filled with people who can think fast and change the plan to fit the need." David looked at Donna for a response.

Donna seemed satisfied so David moved on to appoint the stake out teams and so on. "When we are staking out a place where we think Dante and his men are we will need to be very careful and discrete. The last thing we want is to have to rescue you. Everyone was in agreement to be careful.

Donna raised her hand again. "I would like to be on one of these stakeouts, David. I think I could do it and it sounds like fun." She looked around at everyone. "What? Don't you think I could do it?"

David raised one eyebrow, "You could do it Donna, but what if the situation gets compromised and you become the victim?"

Donna looked around, "Ah, you think I can't make good quick decisions. Please David, I can do this." Donna pleaded.

Bob was concerned. "Donna we are dealing with a ruthless killer. Not the neighborhood bully. Maybe you should be here at the base helping pull us all together." Bob smiled and rubbed Donna's shoulder.

"No!" Donna was determined to be a part of the stakeouts and no one could talk her out of it. She crossed her arms in determination.

Everyone started grumbling. David held up his hands, "Quiet!" he yelled. "We'll put Donna on stakeout team one. If she doesn't work out and they have time they can deliver her back here to base. Is that agreeable?" David looked for agreement. Everyone nodded their head.

Glenn looked at the teams. "Hey, that's my team. Shouldn't we be able to say no?"

David looked down at his lists. "No, I've assigned the teams and I don't really have the time to argue with you.

Donna raised her hand again, "I don't want to be on a stakeout team. I changed my mind. I'll just stay here and help the base team."

"Okay." David said with a big sigh. "No more changes it goes down like the plan. Team one is Glenn, Al, Augie, and Dusty. Team two is, Vic, Terri, Cindy and Bill. Team three is, Dave, Harley and Bob. Team four is, Debbie, Joann, Carol, and Karen. Base Team is, Harold, Dorothy, Barbara, Donna and Phyllis. Our Special Force is Gene, Marlene, Pastor Gerry, and Norma. Then I thought we could use someone in Mobil Park City, so I want Sheriff Archie and Maxine to return home and get with Willy and Virg." Everyone grumbled. David frowned at them. "Hold it guys, quiet!" The grumbling slowly stopped. "Sheriff Archie apologized for all his wrong doing and Maxine was innocent. She didn't even know what he was up to. So it's time we forgave and give them a chance to redeem themselves. I'm adding Willy and Virg to the list as well. Do you have anymore complaints?" David looked around at everyone. "I don't want anyone hurt, so if you get into a jam call for help. I have a radio for every one of the teams. We'll send out a scout first, that's me. Once I have made a visual I'll call in a team. It depends on the situation as to which team I will call, so be ready to roll at a moments notice. I want to place each team in a different place around the area I believe Dante might be. Team one watch his house, the address is on your team sheet, don't loose it. Team two I want you to watch the marina at Canyon Lake. Team three, watch the club he frequents, again it's on your sheet. Team four please watch the highway going into Mobil Park City. The Special Force will stay here at base until we locate your look-alikes.

David and all the teams got into the limo to go locate some cars. "Do you think we should rent some cars to be safe?" asked Vic.

"No." David answered as he drove down the dirt road. "We will get some agency cars. They can't be traced back to you personally."

Harley spoke up. "Why don't we go to the agency with this and have them flush out Dante and his crew?"

David looked in the rearview mirror. "I have addressed the agency with these matters. They haven't been able to catch up with Dante for years. I offered them my idea and they thought it might work. We flush him out and they capture him."

Vic brushed his hair back. "If they haven't been able to catch up with him what makes you and the agency so sure we can?"

Harley chimed in, "Yea and in agency cars."

David smiled, "First of all the agency cars look like a regular car. You don't get the good ones. And he already tried to kill you. He's been running jobs with four look-alikes from our city so he must think we are pushovers. I personally think we have the best chance to catch him."

Bob laughed, "I guess we are the guinea pigs. Does the agency have a copy of our outlined plan?"

"No, I didn't want to let them know all we were doing. It's for our safety." David was serious.

Al sat quietly in the back of the limo with his head hanging down. "All I wanted to do was hunt some treasure, not fight bad guys."

Vic smiled, "It comes with the territory Al. We've now had two different groups after us. What else can happen?"

Dave looked around. "Don't ask. I for one don't want to know."

Harley laughed. "Let's just catch these guys and try again."

Al looked at everyone. "You want to keep trying?"

Joann laughed, "Yes, we haven't had this much fun in years."

Al perked up with this news. David reached the deserted airfield and approached the hanger where the cars would be waiting for them. "I'm going to take a look inside dad. Climb into the drivers seat so if something happens you get everyone out of here."

Dave got out of the passenger side of the limo and walked around to the driver's side. David got out too. "Be careful son. If you don't open the door in say, five minutes or less, I'll drive away. Do you think that should be enough time?" Dave shook David's hand.

David looked around, "Yes, I think so."

Debbie stepped out of the back of the limo. "Why don't some of us who can move quickly take a look around the outside of the building?"

Harley stuck his head out of the door. "I think that's a good idea. What do you think David?" He asked as he stepped out of the limo too.

David shook his head. "You guys are better than my agents, and much more ambitious. It's a great idea, dad you Harley and Vic take a look around. Mom, drive the car. I think you will know if you need to change the plan or not." David turned and walked to the door of the hanger. Dave went around the building one-way and Harley, and Vic took off around the building the other way.

Debbie got into the drivers seat of the limo. "Oh no!" exclaimed Augie. "You aren't going to go crazy on us are you?"

Debbie looked around in the back of the limo. "Only if the situation calls for it." She laughed.

David entered the hanger. They sat in the limo looking around waiting for David to open the door or Dave, Harley, and Vic to come back. It felt like twenty minutes but was only ten when the door of the hanger opened. Debbie looked at David to make sure it was okay to drive the limo into the hanger. David motioned to her to enter. Debbie drove the limo into the hanger and parked it.

They all got out of the limo relieved and started talking. David held up his hand to quiet them. "Shhh." David whispered. "Where are dad, Harley, and Vic?"

Debbie looked towards the door. "They aren't back yet."

David looked stern. "I want everyone to take everything we do seriously from now on. Don't make noise unless it is needed. Bob take the green car and drive it around to find dad and the others. Mom your team takes the blue car and go the opposite direction of Bob. Make sure those guys are found and they get in with Bob. Oh wait a minute; Vic needs to get into the car with Bill and Cindy. Bill you take the black car and pick up Vic. Just follow Bob. Glenn your team can take the tan car. As soon as everyone is in the right car get out of here and go to your designated stakeouts. I'll be in contact so turn on your radios to channel two." They all got into their cars and took off.

David took a jeep and headed back to locate Dante. Bob and Bill drove around the buildings until they returned back to the front of the hanger where they found Dave, Harley and Vic. David was gone and had locked up the hanger. They all headed off to their stakeout

Locations.

# CHAPTER 24

*David thought* Dante would be at his house so he headed there. Even though Team one was to stakeout the house David wanted to confirm Dante's position first. Sure enough he was at his house. David parked his jeep in a dark alley. Then he slipped out into the darkness and to the wall that surrounded Dante's house. Once on top of the wall, he thought about dogs. "Oh. What if there are dogs." David reached into his pack for a dog whistle and sure enough he had one. Relieved David blew the whistle to see if he would get a response. Nothing, once again he blew the whistle and not one dog showed up. Not even a bark. Either the rumor of Dante hating dogs was true or he had deaf dogs. David decided to risk it. Over the wall he went creeping through the dark until he came to the house.

Looking through the window to see if there was some activity, David saw two men walking into a room and shutting the door. He moved around the house and came to a window that revealed the room the men walked into. There was Dante, two of his men and the four look-alikes of Mobil Park City. David looked around and found a trellis to climb up where he could look into the window and see what was on the desk the people were looking at. It was another job for the look-alikes. David took out his binoculars and studied the plans. He then climbed down and slipped away into the dark. Climbing the wall he noticed the stakeout car. David went straight to his jeep. Once inside he radioed Team one.

David spoke in a low voice. "Team one, come in."

Al answered, "This is team one."

David confirmed Dante was in the house. "Dante is in the house and the four look-alikes are in there too. They are planning a caper. It's the Newby Bank in Heavenly. I want you to stay here and watch the house. If a car should leave don't follow. Wait there will be another car leave not long after the first. Give them a ten minute start, you already know where they are going so don't hurry just drive to Heavenly. Once you arrive wait on the east side just before entering town. I think there is a place you can park and not look conspicuous. I'm leaving for Heavenly now. I'll contact you once I know what we need to do." David took off and drove toward Heavenly. "Come in team two."

Cindy answered, "This is team two."

David told them the same thing he told team one except he wanted them to go into town and park in a used car lot across the street from the bank. "Come in team four." David called.

Joann answered, "We're here but Debbie decided we should head for Heavenly."

David laughed, "Leave it to mom to jump at making her own decisions. Okay" David answered "You are going to have to park down the street at the local bar."

"Can we walk down to the bank?" Joann asked laughing.

David sighed, "I told you to be serious."

Joann giggled some more. "We are I just can't help myself."

David took on a serious mood again. "No stay in the car until you hear from me. Come in Base."

Harold answered the radio. "This is base."

David was anxious to get the special force to Heavenly before the look-alikes arrived. "I need the special force here in Heavenly now. They need to meet me a block east of the Newby Bank."

Harold relayed the message to Gene, Marlene, Pastor Gerry and Norma. They left immediately for Heavenly. "Scout, this is base team. Special force is on their way."

David acknowledged Harold's answer. Dave was wondering what they should do. "Scout, this is team three where do you want us?"

David checked his map and then answered Dave. "I want team three to stay put. Dante may arrive at the club while his friends do the job for him."

"Okay" came Dave's answer. Team four sat back and watched the activity around the club.

David was amazed to see special force arrive in record time. "Team two have the pigeons arrived yet?"

Cindy, Bill, Terri and Vic had been talking among themselves. Terri answered. "No, we were wondering if you have someone watching the back of the bank."

David returned her call with yes he was watching the back of the bank. "Team four drive down the street and turn the corner by the bank. If no one is around as you drive by the alley slow down and have a look. Be careful. Then park on the block on the back side of the bank."

Joann eagerly said, "Will do Scout." Debbie drove down the street and turned the corner slowing down as she passed the alley. No one saw a thing. Joann reported to David as they continued to circle the block and park on the backside of the bank. David instructed the special force to remain in the car and out of sight. He instructed them to pay attention to all activity around them and wait for his call.

It wasn't long when a van drove down the street in front of the bank and around the corner. Team two got excited as Terri reported the van to David. By that time David had entered the alley and positioned himself in a dark corner to watch and wait. He spotted the van as it drove into the alley. David watched intently. It was dark but he could make out two men getting out of the van. As the van left down the alley the men climbed the bank wall and disappeared over the top. David called team four. "Team four, a van just drove down the alley leaving two men do you see it?" David waited and watched for the men to return.

Terri answered, "The van is circling this direction, they just passed us and turned the corner again."

David looked toward the street. Sure enough the van passed the alley and drove down the street.

Just about that time Joann spoke up. "I see the van and it's turning down the street we are parked by." They were all silent for a moment.

Debbie, Joann, Carol and Karen ducked down as the van drove slowly by. Carol peeked up to see if it was clear. "Get up, it passed us and is turning up the street towards team two." Carol whispered.

Joann started giggling and before they knew it they were all giggling. "I feel silly." Joann giggled.

"Shh." Debbie hushed them. Pretty soon they heard David on the radio.

"Is the van going to stop or keep driving?" David was asking team two. The van drove by them again.

"I don't know." Came Terri's answer. "Wait, oh no, they are pulling into the used car lot. What should we do?" Came a panicked cry from Terri.

David said as calm as he could. "Duck down and cover up with blankets. Be quiet and still. One of you should check out where they are parking."

Terri's voice was such a quiet whisper you almost couldn't hear her. "They are parking right next to us." She sounded a little panicked. "What do we do?"

David told them to sit tight until help came. "Team four, this isn't an easy task. I want you to drive down the street and circle around so you can't be seen by the van. Get as close to the used car lot as possible. Let me know when you are in place. Special team, you're up as well move as undetected as possible and get over to where team four is. Tell me when you're there." David continued to watch for the two men.

After about five minutes team four and special force reported they were both parked just down the side street from the used car lot. David was hoping just the two women were in the van. "You need to figure out how to approach the van and apprehend the two women and who ever else is in the van. I hope there is only two women." David said nervously. "If we fail we could be in worse trouble than we are now. Team two as soon as you hear commotion you need to help the other two teams."

They all answered with, "It's a go." Team four and special force crept up the street to the used car lot. Spotting the van they made their way over as close as they dared. "What do we do now?" Asked Marlene.

Debbie thought for a moment. "I have it, Gene you go over like you are the other Gene. If they don't see you then you are good and can catch them by surprise. However if they do catch you then you need to act like you forgot something. Try to confuse the issue." Debbie looked worried.

Gene stared at Debbie. "You've got to be kidding surely. They will catch on to that. Don't you have a better idea?"

"No. I think it will work for a moment and that's when Pastor Gerry will creep up on the other side of the van and open the door surprising them. The rest of us will go after that. With a lot of luck and whatever else is needed, maybe we will capture the van and the two women look-alikes." They all looked at Debbie like she had lost her mind. "We can't afford to blow this guys. If you have a better idea tell me please. Otherwise we have to make this work. Our lives depend on it."

Gene adjusted the waistband of his pants like he was mustering up some courage. "Okay here I go." Off he went to the van.

Debbie watched shaking her head. "I hope this works. Go Pastor Gerry so you are up there in time to aid Gene." Pastor Gerry made his way to the van. Gene had their attention for a second. Pastor Gerry's entrance was just in time and surprised them good. The rest of the teams and special force all came down on the van. The two women were apprehended. The van was checked over for more people and none were found.

Debbie radioed David, "our mission is accomplished." She turned to Marlene and Norma, "Quick Marlene, you and Norma change clothes with these women and get in the van." Debbie suggested. Then turned to the two women. "Alright, how are you to know when to drive back to the alley?" Questioned Debbie in a gruff voice.

Carol looked stunned. "Debbie, I've never seen you so mean."

Joann grabbed one of the women by the nap of the neck. "You better answer or else."

Karen looked stunned as well. "Are we going to hurt them?"

Joann, Carol and Debbie all said, "Yes!"

Carol laughed, "Well not if they tell us all we need to know about the robbery and where to meet up with Dante."

Terri, Cindy, Bill and Vic were astonished as well but stood there just watching. They finally got the information out of the women. Terri spoke up, "Are you sure you got the truth? Maybe you should do something to them anyway just to make sure." Vic and Bill's mouths dropped open. They couldn't believe the women.

Debbie started towards the Marlene look-alike when she freaked and burst out with different information. "Which is it? The truth or else." About that time David called Vic and told him the agency was sending a car for the two look-alike women. He was relieved and told the others that help was on the way. They were all relieved to part with the two look-alike women.

Marlene and Norma got into the van and waited for the men in the bank to signal them to return. Pastor Gerry and Gene got into the back of the van with Vic, Debbie, Joann and Carol. The rest stayed put in their vehicles until David called them and told them to move.

Marlene was getting nervous. "What if the men know we aren't the right women? This could back fire on us bad."

Debbie was right behind Marlene's seat. "Don't worry Marlene, we will apprehend the men before they get to even talk to you." She patted Marlene's shoulder and crouched down again.

About that time the men radioed Marlene and Norma to pick them up in the alley. Marlene freaked. "What do we do?"

Norma took a deep breath. "Marlene!" She sternly said. "Quiet, I'll answer."

Debbie quickly said, "No!"

Vic looked at Debbie, "Why shouldn't she answer."

"I don't know, wait until they call again. Slowly start driving around to the alley to pick them up. We might not need to answer. If we do it might alarm them that something is up. Maybe they have a code." Debbie started thinking. "If they call again repeat what the pretend Norma said when we were grilling her about what the plan was."

Joann leaned forward. "What if she was lying? We didn't have much time to grill her on the plan."

Marlene panicked, "What do we do we're entering the alley!"

Debbie grabbed her arm. "Settle down, we apparently are doing okay or they would have called us by now. Just drive down the alley and David will signal us to stop when we reach the approximate place they stopped before. Go slow and don't panic. If they call we're all here with you. We'll figure this out as we go." Debbie calmed herself down and slid down behind the seat. Everyone got down low except Marlene and Norma. David radioed Debbie as they slowly reached the place to stop.

"Stop slowly Marlene." Marlene slowly came to a stop.

The men radioed Marlene and Norma thinking still they were the two look-alikes, to see if it was clear to approach. Norma cleared her voice and practiced talking like her look-alike. "Clear, come on." Norma took a deep breath. "Did I sound okay?"

"Yes" they all whispered from the back of the van. By this time Debbie and the others had moved to the very back of the van incase the men opened the side door to enter.

The men approached the van. Marlene and Norma tried to act like they thought the other women would act in the situation. One of them waved and Marlene motioned for him to hurry. They opened the side door and entered the van closing the door behind them. Marlene hit the gas while Vic and the others in the back of the van grabbed the men. Marlene drove back to the used car lot as fast as she could go taking curves on two wheels.

Debbie yelled, "Slow down Marlene!" as she came flying over the back seat headfirst. Grabbing the front passenger seat back, Debbie managed to pull herself up and turned to slap both the men posing as Gene and Pastor Gerry. About that time Marlene slid into a parking place by Vic's car where they had been waiting. Terri, Cindy, Bill and the others were shocked to see the van come in so fast and sliding into the parking space. They almost panicked when they saw the van coming right for them.

By that time Vic, the real Gene and Pastor Gerry had the men relieved of weapons, stolen goods and bound up with handcuffs David had furnished them. "Wow", Joann and Carol sat down in the back of the van.

Debbie climbed in the back with them. "You're telling me. I didn't like the ride at all. Do I drive like that?" before they could answer, Debbie changed her mind in wanting to know. "On second thought don't answer."

Joann and Carol laughed. "Oh Debbie, you drive worse." Joann giggled. "However I have come to realize crazy driving is a must in hunting treasure or running from bad guys." The back door of the van opened and Joann climbed out. Debbie sat there frowning.

Carol climbed out the back of the van too. "I have heard about your driving and I don't know after this ride if you are worse or the same as Marlene when it comes to driving."

David finally arrived and shortly after he came to the used car lot the agents from the agency arrived. After a short discussion with the agents, David walked over to the van where the look-alike men were being held. "We need to talk with the men and women so the rest of you except Marlene, Gene, Pastor Gerry and Norma don't need to be present. Get into your cars and wait until we decide what to do next. Thank you, you're a great team to work with." David smiled at them and they all got into their cars and waited.

Glenn, Al, Augie and Dusty decided not to stay at the east end of town so they drove up to the used car lot where all the action was. Getting out of the car Al and Dusty stayed with David to make sure all went well.

"First we want to know where you are supposed to meet Dante. What was your plan?" David looked at the men. They weren't in a talkative mood.

Al however was anxious to find his treasure and get on with life. He lunged forward grabbing the Gene look-alike by the collar. "Tell them or I'll…"

David grabbed Al interrupting his obvious aggression. "Al, we don't handle it like that." David moved Al back away from the men.

Al was upset. "How do you handle them?" The men began to snicker at Al.

David turned abruptly and slugged the Pastor Gerry look-alike. "That's how we handle it." The men weren't laughing anymore. "Now tell me what I want to know or I'll do it again."

Al, Dusty and the real Gene and Pastor Gerry were shocked to see David in action as it were. The agents holding the look-alikes were encouraging David to slug the men again when look-alike Gene yelled,

"NO! I'll tell you everything just don't hurt me."

David smiled and nodded to his colleagues. "I'm listening." The two look-alikes told David they were supposed to meet Dante at the marina. They were supposed to bring the loot to the boat.

David asked them if Dante would be on the boat. They both nodded their heads. Then the Gene look-alike added, "By the way just so you know and don't go in blind. Dante has a thing for Maggie."

The real Gene looked stunned. "Who's Maggie?"

David looked at Gene and smiled, "Marlene?" David then looked at the look-alike Gene in question.

"Yep! They have a hot and heavy relationship. Don't say I didn't warn you. If she acts shy or negative Dante will know she's the real one replacing the look-alike." Gene's look-alike smirked.

Gene got mad and backhanded the look-alike. "You weasel!"

David intervened, "Gene, we'll think of something." David turned to the look-alikes. "Is there a time you are supposed to be there before they start getting nervous?"

The Pastor Gerry look-alike started to answer but was interrupted by Gene's look-alike. "No don't answer, you let him hit me."

"Answer or I'll hit you again." The real Gene scowled. The look-alikes exchanged looks with Gene and finally told all they knew.

David was satisfied with what he heard so he instructed the agents to take them away to jail. "What about Marlene?" Gene questioned. "You don't expect her to go into that den knowing what we know. I won't have Marlene put in that position. I forbid it. Besides I don't think I could keep my cool." Gene was agitated about the whole mess.

David calmed Gene down. "No I don't expect to put Marlene in such a position. If I knew she would be okay that would be a different story. I think we will use the look-alike."

"What?" came a shocked response from the others? "What if we can't control her once she is back in with her gang and lover. That would put us in serious jeopardy." Pastor Gerry was very worried about the whole plan.

Marlene spoke up. "Look, I think I can do this. Gene will have to play along and we can do this so it doesn't leave us in there long with them."

Gene strongly objected. "No! What if you have to kiss him or he puts his hands on your butt or something worse! No, I won't have it. I can't control myself." Gene lit up a cigarette, and started pacing.

David walked over to Gene snatched the cigarette out of his lips and put a firm hand on his shoulder. "Gene, we will try to control the situation and I think if you don't look at Marlene when you arrive it will be better. You have to cope. I think Pastor Gerry is right we may not be able to control the look-alike Marlene once you get in and that could be bad for all of you. We'll swarm the boat once you enter and knock off the guards. Then we'll try to enter the cabin by surprise once that's done. It may take a minimum of ten to fifteen minutes. Can you pretend for that long, Gene?"

Gene stood there staring at David. Then he looked at Marlene. "Okay, but you better hurry and don't make us wait long. And you Marlene don't be coquettish. Just go fix coffee or get him a drink to stay away from him." Gene was frustrated but knew it was the best plan.

David called Team three, his dad's team. "Dad, are you still at the Club?"

Harley answered, "Yes we are, do you have something else for us to do? We're getting bored here listening to your activity."

David informed team three the look-alikes had been apprehended. He also told them they were on their way to the marina to meet up with Dante. "I want you to go to the marina we will be needing some backup and it would be nice to have more men."

They all laughed, "What's wrong David, are the women getting out of control?" Harley asked.

"Just tell dad he has the makings of a real live interrogator in mom. I think she was enjoying herself for a moment." David laughed.

Dave took the radio, "sounds like your mom. We'll be at the marina and ready to help."

David and some agents got into the van with Gene, Marlene, Pastor Gerry and Norma. Gene was driving. "Take us to the marina and park in a dark place. Observe the area when you drive in so you are aware of the men Dante has watching the area." David instructed.

Dave, Harley, and Bob drove to the marina as well. After about twenty minutes the other teams began to drive to the marina in ten-minute increments. Upon arriving at the marina Gene, and his colleagues studied the area. He drove up to the marina and parked in a dark area not far from the dock they would walk down to the boat. Gene and the others were nervous. "We're here." Gene said in a quiet voice. "Now what?"

David looked up over the seat. "Get out and walk to the boat carrying the bags. It's all fly by the seat of your pants from here." David patted Gene's arm. "Good Luck!" David ducked down again.

Gene, Marlene, Pastor Gerry and Norma exited the van carrying the bags. "From out of the dark came a voice. "Hello!" They looked off toward some trees. The four became nervous.

David perked up. "What?" He whispered.

One of his agents looked out toward the trees with his night vision glasses. "Dante sir. He's not on the boat. What now?" Whispered the agent.

David looked out too. Sat down and thought for a moment and then looked out again. David took his night vision glasses out and scanned the area around the entrance. "Ted" David whispered. "Do you see Gene and company?" Ted looked out and saw Gene and company walking over to the trees and Dante.

Gene was nervous. Marlene knew it would be up to her to try and save the situation. "Baby, you aren't on the boat." Marlene was trying to talk like the look-alike, sort of trashy southern. She walked up to Dante and wrapped her arms around him. "Is something wrong sugar?"

Dante grabbed Marlene and held her close looking into her eyes and such. "Ya" he replied then pushed her away. Marlene almost lost her balance. She was wearing tall heels and a very short skirt. Not the most comfortable.

Gene was so nervous Marlene's performance went by the way side. "Why the change in plans?" Pastor Gerry threw the bag he was carrying down on the ground at Dante's feet and then retrieved the one Norma was carrying and did the same with it.

Dante looked at the bags. Gene had been carrying two bags as Marlene didn't carry one at all. He placed the bags down with the others. "I got information you might be followed." Dante motioned for some of his guys to retrieve the bags. "Were you followed?"

Marlene just stood there. Gene looked at Dante, "No I don't think so. We used the usual switch we always use. You're getting nervous in your old age Dante." Gene watched the men haul off the bags into the dark. "You aren't putting them on the boat?"

Dante stared at Gene. "No, we're leaving for Mobil Park City. There's a sheriff I want to talk to." He smiled.

Gene studied the man. "Why do you want to see the sheriff of Mobil Park City?"

Dante smiled again. "He needs to know he has some real bad citizens living in his town."

Gene smiled, "Oh, arresting our look-alikes. Good idea, then we can go back to their houses and live there."

"No, stupid." Dante was suddenly agitated. Gene became angry. He didn't like being called stupid. "If they're arrested then you can't go live there. You need to disappear."

Pastor Gerry became alarmed. "Disappear? You mean leave the country don't you?"

Dante laughed his wicked laugh. "No, you are stupid too. I mean we are going to eliminate you now because you are a liability to me." Dante looked at the three of them, Gene, Pastor Gerry, and Norma. Then he turned around looking for Marlene. She wasn't there. In her nervous state she disappeared into the dark. Dante's men didn't do anything because the fake Marlene usually did the same thing. "Where's toots?"

One of Dante's men answered, "She went back there somewhere."

Dante was agitated again. "Why didn't you stop her?"

Another man of Dante's answered. "Cause she always wanders off. We didn't think anything of it."

Dante was angry. "Go find her now and bring her to the boat." The men left to go find Marlene. Dante took Gene, Pastor Gerry and Norma to the boat. In the mean time David was trying to figure out how to get out of the van undetected by Dante or his men. The perfect moment had finally arrived. While Dante's men were looking for Marlene and Dante was taking the others to the boat they had a chance to get out of the van.

Once out of the van David looked around. "Do you see any of the men that went into the dark by the trees?" No one answered. Just about that time David saw his dad in the trees waving to him. He looked around and then ran over him. "What are you doing dad?"

Dave had Vic, Harley and Al with him not to mention Marlene. David was surprised. "We eliminated Dante's men and your agents have them now. All we have to do is collect Gene and company."

"You know I think you guys should have been agents. You're good." David looked back at his men waiting for him in the shadows by the van. "They took the others to the boat. I think Dante has three other men with him. You must have captured the rest." David thought for a moment. "You take Marlene out of here and get safe. My agents and I will rescue Gene and company and hopefully capture Dante and the rest of his men. Thanks, guys." David ran back to his agents who were waiting by the van.

Dave watched as David and his agents made their way to the boat. Then he told Vic, Harley, Al and Marlene to go get in the car and he would meet them back up at the entrance. "No." Vic whispered. "If you're going to help so are we." They all nodded their heads.

Al chuckled quietly, "You know this is more exciting than hunting treasure. It's even more rewarding."

Harley laughed, "I think you are crazy, finding treasure would be more fun and rewarding in a monetary way."

Dave hushed them "Let's position ourselves by the dock entrance. If Dante and his men escape David they would have to come by us to get away. Come on let's go." Dave, Vic, Al, Harley and Marlene took off running through the dark to make their way over to the entrance of the marina dock Dante's boat was at. They stayed in the dark shadows and behind a shack that was near by.

Vic was breathing heavy. "What now?"

Dave peeked around the corner. "We wait until David makes his move. We need to stay alert so don't get comfortable."

Harley sighed, "I don't think we can. With bad guys out to get us and all."

Marlene was impatient so she walked around the back of the shack and could see something happening in the boat. Running back around to where Dave and the others were she was excited. "I think something is happening on the boat!" She was so excited she almost passed out.

Dave and the others ran around the back of the shack and saw through the windows of the cabin on the boat. There was some ruckus going on but what exactly Dave couldn't make out. Harley, Vic and Al peeked around the shack too. "Oh" they said in unison

They heard some shots and jumped back. Then ran back to the side of the shack and looked toward the boat from that direction. Marlene was jumping up and down. "What do you think? Should we go in and help?" Another shot rang out. "Oh" Marlene groaned in concern.

Dave, Vic, Harley, and Al looked around the shack. The view was obstructed by another large boat. Then they heard running. Dave squatted way down close to the ground and crawled to the other side of the entrance. About that time Dante came running out. Vic, Al, Harley and Dave jumped him and Marlene in desperation grabbed a floatation ring off the shack and stuck it over the top of him. Dave and the others helped the floatation ring go down on him penning his arms down. They had captured Dante.

Vic shoved Dante back behind the shack and Al and Harley hung on to him. Dave backed off to the other side of the entrance again. The next to arrive was David and his agents. They had successfully captured Dante's men and freed Pastor Gerry, Norma and Gene. Marlene was so happy to see Gene in one piece.

The agents collected Dante and his men and carted them off to jail. Debbie and the others drove down to the marina and parked jumping out of their cars and cheering David, Dave, the agents, Vic, Harley, Marlene, Pastor Gerry, Norma and Gene. "Where have you been?" Dave asked Debbie and the others.

Debbie laughed. "We decided you could handle these guys. So we waited at the highway incase one got away and tried to escape. Good work guys."

David watched everyone celebrating the triumphant win. "Hey, we still have a treasure to find. Do I have any takers?" They all turned to David and yelled, "Yes!"

## CHAPTER 25

*Debbie heard* the birds as she opened her eyes. It was early dawn and the sun hadn't quite come up yet. Rubbing her eyes she got up and walked over to the window. It was going to be a good day. There would be no one chasing or shooting at them. She smiled as she woke Dave up. "Hey, big guy, get up and greet the day." Debbie kissed Dave on the cheek as he woke up.

He smiled at her. "What are you cooking up for the day?" he asked her.

"Did you forget we are going to hunt treasure today?" Debbie laughed.

Dave had forgot. "Oh, you are right we are. What time is David picking us up?"

Dave rushed to get ready. "He'll be here at seven sharp." Debbie told him as she hurried to get ready too. Time rushed and soon David arrived to get them.

Out the door they ran making sure they had their packs. "Good morning David." Debbie was in a good mood.

David smiled, "You must have had a good nights sleep."

Dave and Debbie looked at each other. "We did."

Dave shut the door of the car. "Where to?"

David looked at his dad. "We are going to meet everyone at the library so we can discuss our plan of action."

Debbie sighed. "Why must we discuss the plan? We know where to look now so we should just go and look." She giggled.

"Mom, we talked about this. If we don't lay some ground rules down then we could later find ourselves in trouble." David was frustrated and it was early.

Debbie patted his shoulder as he drove. "Okay, I know, it's a good idea just ignore me."

David looked in the rearview mirror. "I will." They arrived to the library and no one was there yet. Debbie hurried up the stairs and unlocked the door. Dave and David parked the limo on the street and went in too. It wasn't long until the others started arriving. When they were all there David had them all seated. "As you all know we are here to go on a treasure hunt. I have outlined some important facts we need to keep in mind when searching for said treasure. Stick together, be quiet, and the big one, don't take more than you can safely carry. If you do take too much it puts the rest of us in danger. So please keep in mind the rules. Do I have discussion?" David looked around the room at the eager faces.

Al raised his hand. "Excuse me, do I have anything to say about this venture? It was my map, wasn't it?"

David smiled. "It was your map until mom found the second map and journal. There's still some confusion about where yours leads but mom and I have a theory that your map was lost somehow and buried. That's how it ended up in your mom's cellar. The map my mom found had a journal and that helps us to decipher the symbols. So we came up with what we think is the place where the treasure could be. We aren't discarding your map yet Al. We are just looking where it is the easiest right now. Does that answer your question?" David looked at Al for an answer. He nodded his head. "If there isn't any other questions than I say we get started." They all went out and loaded into the limo.

Dave rode up front with David. "Are you sure this limo will get to the place we need to be?" asked Vic.

David laughed. "I think so we'll just have to see."

After driving for a couple hours David turned off onto a dirt road. "Hey, we're going to Trepid Falls." Vic announced. "What makes you think the treasure is buried there?"

Debbie got out the map. "It's the honeycomb on the map, see."

Joann looked at the map. Debbie passed it around to everyone. "I thought it was in Pilot Cove or Marble Point. When did you decide to go to Trepid Falls?"

Debbie took the map and put it back in her pack. "David and I believe it could be in the under water cave instead of Canyon Lake."

Donna spoke up. "You don't suggest we go swimming do you?"

Debbie looked at Donna. "That's the only way in. If you don't want to go swimming you will miss out on all the excitement and treasure." She giggled.

Joann was eager. "I think it'll be fun."

Dorothy was a bit hesitant as well. Harold shook his head. "I'm to old to go swimming in cold water."

Vic laughed, "What do you mean, you went swimming in cold water when you escaped from David's boat just before it blew up."

Harold laughed too. "I know and it was a good thing we did or we wouldn't be here now."

Donna thought for a moment. "I think we should all stick together this time. I don't want to get kidnapped again. It was awful. Worse than the cold water we had to swim in."

They finally arrived to Trepid Falls. David announced, "We're here. Take your packs and head for the falls. I'll catch up with you."

Dave looked at David, "Why aren't you coming now?"

David explained he wanted to move the limo to a secure place and make sure it was hidden just incase there were some surprises. Dave acknowledged his reasoning and shut the door. Everyone headed down the path to Trepid Fall's pool. When they arrived they sat down to wait for David. It wasn't long until he arrived.

David looked at the eager faces waiting for him to direct their steps. He motion for Al to come up and join him and Dave. Al was happy to do so. "Today we are going to hunt for a treasure." David announced. "Thanks to Al finding the first map and mom the second we now have two chances of finding treasure. That's quite exciting especially this day and age. Most treasures have been found or buried forever. I strongly recommend we all stay together and that means we all get wet and miserable together. I for warned all of you about the conditions this adventure held for us and I'm sure there could be some unforeseen conditions ahead. Hopefully we have laid the map-seeking goons to rest once and for all but you never know. We need to be alert at all times and don't take anything for granted. With that in mind did you all bring your goggles with you?" David observed that they had brought all the things he listed for them to bring. "Okay lets get started. Mom and dad have been to this cave under the falls so I think I will take them and discuss how to get there in the mean time Al will divide you all into three groups. Go ahead Al." David got with Dave and Debbie to learn the approach to the cave. Debbie had been the last person to go to the cave and the most recent. "Has the entrance to the cave changed at all since you and dad were there a few years ago?" questioned David.

Debbie took a piece of paper and drew some sketches for Dave and David. "Yes it has changed a little. The current is much stronger pushing you away from the entrance. It is also deeper than I remembered it being."

Dave studied Debbie's drawing. "Can we approach from the other side?" Dave asked Debbie.

"No we can't, it looks like there must have been a mud slide of some kind. The entrance is smaller and harder to find than it was previously. I'm not even sure the area is stable as it is. There could be another slide and close off the entrance for good." Debbie explained.

Dave and David studied the drawing and land around the falls. Debbie walked around with them. "What if we enter the water here by the falls it would save swim time and we could get to the entrance quicker." Dave suggested.

Debbie disagreed to his suggestion. "It won't work. You need to approach from a distance of at least twenty feet. If we enter the water from over there, straight across from the falls as I did we have a better chance of getting to the entrance without incident. You have to swim through the current to the entrance there's no other way. To approach from your suggested area we potentially could start another slide and someone could get hurt or die." She looked at Dave and David and then looked at the people with them. "Let's face it guys, these people aren't all that athletic or in shape. We need to find a way so they can go but not get hurt."

David smiled like his mom smiled when she had a wild idea. "I think I know what will help. I have over four hundred feet of climbing rope. I told everyone to bring a ten-foot piece of rope with them. We tie a loop in the four hundred foot rope about every five feet. Then everyone will take their rope and tie it around their waist. At the other end we attach the carabineer I told them to bring and hook onto the main rope where we made a loop. No one gets lost and if they have difficulty swimming through the current we pull them through. Put two strong swimmers in front of four weak swimmers and so on. I think that will work to insure safety." David felt he had a good plan.

Dave thought about the suggested plan. "I think it can work. I think we need to have a break between groups swimming to the cave though in case there is a problem of any kind." Debbie and David agreed and everyone was comfortable with the plan. They suggested the plan to everyone else and it was unanimously agreed upon.

Al announced the groups. "In Debbie's group I put Joann, Vic, Marlene, Gene, Pastor Gerry and Norma. In Dave's group I put Bob, Donna, Cindy, Glenn, Karen and myself. In David's group I put Carol, Harley, Harold, Dorothy, Phyllis, and Augie. I think Dusty and Terri can bring up the end. What do you think?"

David thanked Al for his help. "Debbie's group will go first because she is the last person to have gone into the cave and it wasn't that long ago. She knows the way." Al grumbled. "Is there something you want to say Al?" David asked.

Al looked around. "Yes, I found the map and so I should at least get to go in the first group."

David laughed. "Okay Al, you can trade places with one of the couples in mom's group." Al was apprehensive but finally traded places with Pastor Gerry and Norma. David told them how they were going to go and informed them of the dangers in not keeping up and not to panic. After the loops were tied in the main rope, Debbie attached her rope to the first loop. David told the groups to decide who in their group were the strongest swimmers. The strongest would go first and last keeping the weakest in the middle in case they needed help.

As soon as Debbie's group was ready she entered the water. "As soon as we enter the water we need to swim as fast as we can to overcome the current and shorten our time in the water. We have no breathing assistance so we need to hold our breath until we reach the cave. I think if we hurry it will be about forty-five seconds. It might be wise to practice holding your breath here first." Everyone practiced holding their breathe for the time suggested. "It is also important to note that when one can't hold their breath they tend to panic. I suggest if you run out of air you swim faster. We will swim out into the middle before we dive down so let's go." Debbie swam out into the pool and the others followed. When she came to the place she intended to dive she made sure everyone was ready to go with her. They dove down into the pool. Debbie swam for all she was worth. It was difficult as she felt some tugging on her rope. Once she had started she needed to continue. The tugging became worse. Debbie swam down and grabbed onto a rock. Turning around she looked toward her colleagues. Karen was fighting the rope and trying to surface. Al was pulling her along the way. Debbie continued and soon came to the entrance. She entered and surfaced in the cave. Soon to follow was Vic and Joann, then Gene and Marlene and finally Karen and Al. They dragged themselves out of the water and unhooked from the main rope. Debbie began to pull the main rope to see if the others had started. Sure enough she got a tug on it. "Quick help me pull the others in." she encouraged Vic and Gene. Al was exhausted from trying to get Karen safely there but got up and helped.

Joann made sure Karen was okay. "I'm okay, I just panicked for a moment. I felt closed in." Karen said out of breath.

Joann was comforting her when the others surfaced one by one. Dave's team did good swimming in. "Of course you did good we did all the work for you." Joann giggled.

Dave felt a tug on the rope. "Hurry and help guys, David's team will need plenty of help Donna could panic." They all rushed to pull in the rest of the party. It was a fast endeavor.

David surfaced and turned around to retrieve Donna who was right behind him. "Oh!" Donna gasped. "That was fun." They all laughed as the rest of the group surfaced.

Al told Donna she had it easy because she didn't have to work as hard as the first group. They all rested for a few moments while Dave and David fixed the main rope for their return.

Karen watched them fix the rope. "You mean we are going to return this way?"

Debbie walked over to Karen. "Yes, we have to there's no other way we know of."

Karen looked around. "Well maybe I can be last like Donna was and get pulled out fast."

Al put his arm around Karen. "I think we can do something about making the return easier on you."

Debbie pulled the map and journal she had found in the cave out of her pack. Laying it down on a big boulder she began to study it and Dave and David joined her. "What now guys, do you have any suggestions?"

Al joined them along with Harley, Vic, Dusty, Terri and Glenn. "I brought my map too." Al pulled his map out and put it up on the rock as well. Debbie showed them the symbol she had found the map and journal behind. They studied the symbol and the maps. Then began looking around the main cave for other symbols or a sign of some kind. Everyone else was sitting around waiting for them to decide where to go from there. As Al, Vic, Glenn, Harley, David, Dave and Debbie walked around looking and studying the walls of the cave Joann and Cindy decided to join the group. Terri and Dusty just sat down and watched them. About that time Al let out a yell and disappeared into the floor of the cave. "Whoa!" exclaimed David.

Karen jumped to her feet and rushed over to where she had seen Al. Dave grabbed her to stop her from entering where Al was. "What do you make of it David?" Dave questioned.

David, Harley, Dusty and Vic were examining the area Al disappeared. All David could say was, "Whoa!" Taking a long expanding rod David carried in his pack he probed the area where Al disappeared. Most of the probing hit solid surface so David moved closer to the middle. He hit a spot in the center of the sand and it collapsed.

They all jumped back. "Who wants to disappear and find Al?" David asked with reservation. By that time they had drawn the attention of everyone there and they were all watching. David looked at everyone.

Karen urged David to do something. "I think we need to be careful there could be another pocket of this kind and we need to be sure Al is okay." Dave suggested.

Harley looked around. "I'll go, I don't mind."

Carol objected strenuously. "No you won't Harley. We don't know if Al is okay. I'm not prepared to loose you here."

Karen was distraught, "Please someone go find Al!"

David hushed everyone. "I'll go."

Debbie got worried. "David isn't there another way?"

"No mom, I think the best bet to find Al right now is to follow him. What do you think dad?" David stood up putting his things into his pack and preparing to go.

Dave gazed at David. "I think you're right unfortunately. Be careful and if you can communicate with us we'll stay here and wait." Dave put his arm around Debbie to comfort her.

Debbie grabbed David's arm. "Be careful son." David nodded.

"Stand back I'll see you soon." With that David stepped into the area where Al disappeared. Everyone watched David disappear into the sand.

Harley was fascinated as was Glenn, Vic, Dusty especially, and some of the others. They watched for a sign from David but nothing happened. "What do we do now? It's been twenty minutes Dave." Harley was anxious to know what happened to the two men.

Dave stood there with Debbie staring at the place Al and David disappeared. "I don't know unless we all follow them." Dave looked up at Harley and the others.

It was quiet for another five minutes. Everyone was thinking about the outcome and entering the area of disappearance. Dave told Harley to mark the area and to make sure everyone stayed out of it. Harley and Glenn put rocks around it.

Dave walked around the rest of the cave looking for something he had seen on one of the maps. Debbie had the maps and decided to study them. Dusty and Terri joined her. "Dave!" Debbie called. "I think

I have it figured out." Dave and everyone else rushed over to Debbie. "Look" she explained as she placed the maps together on the boulder. We shouldn't be looking for a symbol. This little mark on the maps that looks like a whirlpool. It's the sand pool." Debbie smiled to think she had figured something significant out.

Dusty added. "I've studied this in school. Amazingly the sand doesn't really drop down when something heavy falls through the soft spot. It is a phenomenon that has something to do with magnetism."

Dave studied the maps. "The mark is on both maps. Is this a mark below the pool mark?" Dave was asking himself as he got a magnifying glass out and looked at it closer. "I think it is two or three wavy lines. I don't know." He was slightly frustrated and wondering what happened to Al and his son.

Dusty and the others took turns looking at the marks. "If I can remember right the magnetized sand is usually over an underground river. Al and David probably landed in an underground river and it carried them off somewhere." It sounded like Dusty was getting carried away with his theory. It is amazing how one can suddenly come up with something so profound.

Debbie looked at Dusty. "What else do you think these maps are telling us? What I mean is do you have anymore theories?"

Dusty looked at the maps again. "Uh, no not really."

They all studied the maps again. Glenn was agitated. "Look I'm not one to go running off in just any direction but if we are to find Al and David shouldn't we follow them. I'm not crazy about the sand sucking me up but it does seem to be a way to go."

Harley and Gene were talking. "We have been talking about the possibility of some of us going and finding David and Al. Maybe there's no need for all of us to go." Harley suggested.

Vic didn't like the idea. "I don't think we should rule out all of us going. I am thinking we all need to stick together."

Dave was listening to everyone's suggestions. "Okay guys listen up. I don't think we should split up either. The map is clear that there is something under the sand pool. I say we all go. Maybe we should vote."

Joann stepped forward. "No we shouldn't vote. We should just follow our leader. David was acting like the leader in his absence I think Dave is the leader. We should do what he thinks we should do."

Dave looked around at everyone for an objection. "If there is no more discussion I think we should go follow David and Al. What do you think?"

Everyone agreed so they gathered their packs and approached the area Al and David disappeared. "Now we don't know what to think or expect so it is important that we go one right after the other. Donna and Karen stick close to someone who can help you if there is a struggle. Everyone look out for each other. I'll go first then send a couple women then a man etc. Who feels strong enough to go last?" Vic and Harley both raised their hands. Dave decided to send Dusty at the end. "Don't hesitate for a second when entering the exit zone. We need to stick together and end up as close together as possible." With that Dave turned and entered the exit zone. One after the other they stepped into the exit zone area and disappeared into the sand. Until Dusty the last one did the same.

## CHAPTER 26

"What a rush!" yelled Dusty as he plunged into the underground river and was swept away in the current. Up ahead he could see Dave's flashlight and heads bobbing up and down. Then it was like they dropped off the face of the earth. Suddenly Dusty was hurled over the edge into a pool. He yelled as he flew over and entered the pool.

David and Al had run over to help everyone out of the water. "What took you so long to join us?" David exclaimed.

Dave and the others were glad to get on land again even if it were underground. "We weren't sure we should follow you into questionable ground." Dave answered. "What do you think we should do now?"

David looked at everyone. "Maybe we should allow them to rest for a minute." Dave agreed, as the experience was exhilarating.

Dave, Debbie and David along with Al sat down to look at the maps. "When we were waiting for you to follow us. Al and I looked around this place. It's phenomenal. It could have been an escape route for the Indians when they used the cave. I don't expect we will be leaving this place the way we came." David told his parents.

Karen walked over and joined them. "What do we do now?"

Debbie smiled at Karen. "We better examine the maps again. I don't think the journal will help us now."

Dave helped Debbie spread out the maps. "No entries about this place I suppose."

Debbie shook her head. "No, but these circles close together puzzle me. There's only one that has an arrow in it and it's pointing up. What do you make of it?"

David examined the maps. "I think it goes to Canyon Lake." He smiled at his parents as they both looked at him.

Dave was amazed. "Both maps are the same map. Look, the map Al had has this mark and Debbie's map doesn't. It has to be the treasure. What do you think?" Dave was pleased to think he had figured it out.

David laughed, "You know dad we might make treasure hunters after all. I think we are real close to the treasure."

Al got excited, "I knew they had to be the same. I mean how in the world could we have found two different maps. Shouldn't we get started?" Al was anxious to get going.

Dave and David agreed to get moving. "Listen up everyone. We need to keep moving. I don't think we have very far to go now." David announced to the others. They all got up gathered their packs again and followed David further into the dark unknown.

They had walked about thirty minutes and everyone was getting tired. "How much longer?" Asked Bob.

"I don't know." Came David's answer out of the dark. All they had were flashlights for light. Not everyone was using them though. They wanted to conserve in case they started loosing battery power.

David reached an apparent wall. He checked out the wall both ways. Everyone arrived in the same area and all started flashing their lights around. "It's a dead end here. I think there must be a way to go through this wall." David encouraged. He searched the wall for a good ten-minutes. After that David returned to his dad and mom who were sitting on a rock looking at the map. "What do you think dad?" David asked.

Dave studied the map. "Are you sure we left the pool in the right direction?" Dave looked at David.

"No I'm not sure. Do you think we should return and examine it more?" David was concerned he might have gone the wrong way.

They all studied the map. "Look at the waterfall, what do you see?"

Debbie was seeing something and wanted David and Dave to see it too.

"I don't know what?" answered David.

Dave wasn't sure what Debbie was seeing either. "I'm with David, what?"

Debbie told them to look through the waterfall. "How do we do that?" They asked.

Debbie laughed, "Haven't you ever heard of a hologram? Look through the waterfall."

Karen got excited, "I've heard of holograms." She rushed over to look at the map.

Dave and David stared at the map until they saw what Debbie was talking about. "Yea, I see it, I think." David smiled.

Dave was still trying to see it. "I don't quite get it."

David instructed his dad to look through the waterfall. "Don't look at the waterfall, look through it. You almost have to go blurry eyed to see it dad."

"Oh, I think I see it." Dave stared for a few moments at the map. "I guess we have to go back to the waterfall."

Everyone at once was discouraged. "We weren't told it would be easy folks. Let's go." Vic encouraged. They all got up and started down the path they had come down. Soon they had arrived back to the waterfall.

"What now, David?" Vic asked.

"Everyone rest while dad and I check out the waterfall." David suggested. Al wanted to go with them and so did some of the other guys. So they all swam over to the waterfall and disappeared under it.

Carol got up and watched them go. "What are we to do if they don't come back? Follow them?"

Debbie got up and walked over to the edge of the water. "Yes I think so. What else would we do?"

After waiting about fifteen-minutes Bob and Vic came back. "Come on everybody we found the way." Announced Vic. They all gathered themselves together and followed them through the waterfall. Beyond the falls was a path through a cave that eventually entered a huge cavern. They made their way through the large room and down another long narrow cave. This time they entered a smaller cavern with a river running through it.

Donna sat down. "Oh no I'm tired of getting wet. Can't we do something else?"

Debbie went over to her. "Keep thinking about getting out of here. That would be our treasure for sure."

David and Dave examined the situation and decided they would have to float the river again. No one was happy but it was the only way unless they went back the way they came and there was not really a way to go that direction.

The weary party collected themselves and entered the water together so the ones who were pretty tired could hold onto someone who was doing good. Down the river they went until it emptied into a lake of sorts. Not big but it did have an island in the middle. As they dragged their weary bodies out of the water this time something shiny caught their eyes. They slowly moved toward the light and to their disbelief there before them was the most magnificent sight they had ever seen. They dropped their packs and sat down exhausted and shocked.

Al started to cry, "I never imagined seeing such a sight!"

Harley was stunned and speechless. All they could do was sit there and stare.

The walls of a round cave were all lit up in gold. They didn't even need their flashlights because it was so bright. David stared for a few minutes and then collected himself. "Dad, we need to be going."

Dave looked over at David, "I know but wow! What do we do with this find?"

Debbie got up and walked over to Dave and David. "I think we are supposed to walk through the tunnel of gold. It's our way home."

They looked at her and smiled. "What a treasure. Great to see but you can't take it home with you." David laughed.

Everyone looked at David and joined him in his laughter. "Shall we go guys?" Dave asked.

Glenn approached David, "Are we going to walk through that tunnel of gold?"

David laughed again, "Yes we are Glenn. And have the time of our lives doing it."

Glenn was excited. "If we find a nugget we can carry can we take it?"

Dave and David looked concerned. "I don't know. You might be able to but we don't know how to get out of here. I suspect we will be swimming and the gold will anchor you down so it doesn't look good for us." Dave told Glenn. "I would hate for you to drown for greed."

Everyone heard the conversation and realized the only treasure they would be leaving with was their lives. As they walked through the tunnel of gold they soaked up the vision they beheld. Once in awhile they would pass a nugget that might not weigh them down if swimming so they would pick it up knowing they might have to discard it in the end. They took their time passing through the tunnel.

They finally came to another river. This had to be the way up maybe. David and his dad studied the area and came to the conclusion it must empty into Canyon Lake. Under Canyon Lake to be exact. "You will be needing to hold your breath and as soon as you are thrust into the lake you need to surface. Don't loose your sense of direction. I'll go first so as soon as I surface I'll go back down to help the rest of you. Terri, you and Dusty are good swimmers so you need to go soon after some of the weaker swimmers. If anyone were able to do the same the help would be greatly appreciated. If the gold you picked up holds you down discard it, your life is worth more than gold." David knew this was a crucial part of their journey.

Dave realized David's apparent apprehension. "Don't worry David, I'll be last and it will go okay."

David looked at his dad. "You can't swim any better than most of these people."

Dave smiled, "I know but I have your mother." Debbie was standing there and smiled at David.

With that in mind David jumped into the river and headed home. One after the other everyone entered the water. Dave and Debbie were the last to leave. Debbie stepped toward Dave and tied a rope around his waist. "I don't want to loose you."

Dave hugged Debbie, "Don't worry you won't. Let's go." Into the water they went. They were thrust into the lake like Dave and David suspected. Dave became a little disoriented and started the wrong way.

Debbie quickly pulled him back and they surfaced. Everyone was there bobbing around in the water. Not one person was lost. Debbie and Dave were thankful and so was David.

When all were accounted for they swam ashore. They were in the cove they had been in when they were diving and got interrupted by Dante and his men. That was a long way from the marina and it was getting dark. "What should we do now?" asked Bob.

David told them to gather firewood and they would build a fire to dry themselves off and keep warm. He figured it wouldn't take the rangers long to arrive if they saw a fire. So they did just that. They built a large fire and sang songs and warmed up. The rangers arrived in two boats to investigate the fire. They were all so glad to see them. However the rangers weren't very happy with them. The fire got put out and Dave, Debbie and friends got rescued and brought to the marina. Ranger Hank remembered David and loaned him a bus to take everyone back to Mobil Park City. On the ride home everyone discovered that they all succeeded in taking a few small nuggets with them.

Debbie smiled at Dave, "I'm glad we aren't greedy and our friends aren't either. Life is our finest treasure!"